Animal
Folk Tales
of Britain
and Ireland

**SHARON
JACKSTIES**

ILLUSTRATIONS BY
BEA BARANOWSKA

The
History
Press

For Fiona and Felix

First published 2020
Reprinted 2021

The History Press
97 St George's Place, Cheltenham,
Gloucestershire, GL50 3QB
www.thehistorypress.co.uk

British Library Cataloguing in Publication Data.
A catalogue record for this book is available from the British Library.

ISBN 978 0 7509 9135 3

Typesetting and origination by The History Press
Printed by TJ Books Limited, Padstow, Cornwall

Contents

Acknowledgements

WITH THANKS TO Giles Abbott; Damon Bridge; Fiona Collins; Joe Crane; Jem Dick; Sonia Guinnessy; Halsway Manor, Somerset; Simon Heywood; Lorcan O'Tuathail; Lisa Schneidau; The Shipwreck Centre, Arreton, Isle of Wight; Iris Skipworth; Yvette Staelens.

Most of all I would like to thank Debbie Felber, who *wormed* her way into story sources I never knew existed, shape-shifted into a *mole* amongst archives not available to ordinary mortals, *beavered* away at finding me unusual stories, *squirreled* the best of these away, and *badgered* me into staying as close to the 'originals' as possible!

Foreword

IT'S A LONG road we've shared with wild animals. Our hunter-gatherer ancestors closely observed the creatures of their world either to hunt them, or to hide from them, or to tune into their spiritual teachings. Thus animals have been fellow travellers and helpers on humanity's evolutionary path since the beginning. They not only provided nourishment, they also gave fur, sinew, skin, bone and horn to make clothing, tools, weapons, instruments and artefacts. They were treated with great reverence and thanks was always given for the lives taken. It was also believed that wisdom and power could be found in their unique character, so animal totems were a key part of early cultures.

It's not surprising, therefore, that most early stories were about animals: about how they made the sun, the moon and the stars, how they came to be, how they created the first people, how they brought fire. In this creation mythology people and animals often transform into each other. In their ritual re-enactment of the founding dramas, early human actors would dance their spirit animal to life and so be imbued with its transcendent power.

That early culture is long gone in Britain. Indeed, post-industrial twenty-first-century life seems to be its polar opposite. And yet vestiges of it remain, not only in the enduring attraction of hunting, fishing and blackberry picking, but also in the stories, in the folktales, myths and legends of these islands. In these traditional hand-me-down narratives, animals speak, humans transform into creatures and beasts are often the wise and knowing ones. The tales express our long and undying fascination with the wild beings that share this wondrous world of ours.

In this book Sharon Jacksties has gathered together an outstanding collection of time-honoured animal tales from all parts of Britain and Ireland. She's included a good number of classics and dressed them afresh in new clothes. We hear, for example, about Finn Mac Cumhaill and his beloved deer wife and otherworldly son, Oisin. There are selkie tales from the Western Isles of Scotland and the old Welsh story of how Arthur's men found Mabon, son of Modron, by asking the Ancient Animals. We learn how Arthur's end was hastened by a snake in the grass, how four kings' children were turned into swans, how the nightingale came by its golden voice.

Sharon has also, with the help of her badger-mole-beaver friend, found lesser-known stories and brought them to life in these pages. Here you can read how the spider turned into a wolf, how the princess became a bear, how the redstart brought fire. And so many more. This rich feast of tales is spiced up with enchanting rhymes, song lyrics and old sayings. And in the last chapter she weaves into the tales accounts of rewilding attempts to bring back some of the animals that have died out in Britain – the lynx, crane, boar, sea eagle and wolf. Her love for the creatures of the wild shines through in all of these stories.

Sharon Jacksties is a consummate storyteller and this comes across in her graceful and poetic retelling of these tales. She has a wry sense of humour and an eye for the absurd. In this book she has created a blend of tales highlighting the bizarre quirkiness of the folk tradition as well as the wisdom and insight that lies therein. More than anything, what comes across is her passionate commitment to story and the huge and human compassion she feels for our animal kin. Read this book and it will rub off on you!

Eric Maddern, Cae Mabon, 2020

Introduction

HOW BEWILDERED MY parents must have been, completely uninterested in animals as they were, to have produced two animal-besotted children. Long before becoming a storyteller I was the devotee of every zoo and wildlife organisation within reach, even corresponding as a young child with our famous animal-collecting pundit and author, Gerald Durrell.

The writing of this book, however, has taken me on a very different journey. It is the stories themselves that have bestowed glimpses of why and how some of our native species are better represented than others in what remains of our traditional canon. The questions that arise from traditional stories are, for me, an enhancement of their ability to create wonder. Despite all folk tales (unlike their mythological cousins) having the characteristically clear-cut endings that promote a sense of satisfaction, it is also the absences and omissions that provide a concurrent interest. For instance, it was a surprise to discover that some of our more iconic animals are so under-represented by fictional story. Bears and wolves, for example, are mostly to be found in the recent Germanic imports from the Brothers Grimm. Earlier Norse stories containing these major predators could arguably be later described as British given that although they were first told by incomers, they were heard and repeated by the incumbent population that itself was made up of previous settlers.

My work as a storyteller has involved many years telling to the very young, often in inner cities where children believe that milk originates from a lorry. Yet even three year olds grow wide-eyed with awe and fear at the mention of bears. They have never seen one and their parents and grandparents, many of whom are from all over the world, have probably not seen bears either. How to account for their reaction when the teller, through neither tone nor description, has inferred nothing untoward? Despite much research, only two British bear stories were found in time for publication. 'Bear Skin', rewritten here, is almost certainly Scottish, possibly Norse in origin/influence, yet part of a genre that has produced many forms of this story throughout Britain. Bears have not lived here for more than a thousand years, but this time-warping story happily presents us with a bear ensconced in a palace garden's wheelbarrow!

The bear story that was not included for reasons of space, is a little-known Arthurian tale. The name 'Arthur' means bear and it is no coincidence that this hero of Britain's most important story cycle is represented by this most powerful of animals. Our hero king, most celebrated for uniting a warring land containing some populations ambivalent towards the new religion of Christianity, is given the name of an animal most significant to what by then must have been vestigial pagan beliefs. In Brythonic Celtic pagan mythology, the bear chases away winter and summons the returning sun for the spring equinox. In this story, a huge, unknown young man appears at court from the forest and asks to be knighted. Arthur takes an instant and most uncharacteristic dislike to him and finds excuses to avoid doing this – one being that nobody knows who the youth's father is. At that point a bear breaks out of the menagerie and rushes up into the tower, where the ladies of the court were to be found. Sir Gawain, Arthur's champion, is also there but can do nothing as he is unarmed. The youth wrestles the bear into submission and throws him out of the window. Arthur then has to knight the young man, but maintains his hostility and distance – an implication being that the newcomer is himself half-bear and that Arthur will not tolerate another in his territory.

There is another echo of the mythological divine in 'Bear Skin' in which a father overprotects his virgin daughter, who escapes him by becoming a bear. The peoples of this land once listened to the classical tales brought by Roman invaders and settlers, in which the bear is dedicated to the Virgin Goddess Artemis, who was known to manifest as a bear.

The shape-shifting between human and animal forms, which contributes so much to the magical element in our traditional tales and folklore, derives from the beliefs and shamanic practices of our animistic ancestors. It is cultural memory preserved in story like a fly caught in amber. When sophisticated pantheons of pagan deities evolved, they took on these powers. Some of the best examples of these ancient beliefs can be found in our myriad stories about hares. The ancient Irish hero Oisin pursues one of these creatures into the Other World, only to find her transformed into her true shape and enthroned as a goddess. In a later age, Christianity disempowered these animals by subverting them from agents of the divine into those of evil and witchcraft whence, in their folk tale form, they continue to delighted us with a frisson from the Dark.

Our vast lore of selkie stories – those hybrid beings that are neither wholly human nor wholly seals – testifies to our fascination with both our need and inability to distinguish ourselves from beasts. During these times of increasing concern about our relationship with Nature, there is a growing interest in animals. May this book play a small part in renewing the wonder that is their due and inspire us to contribute to their protection.

Sharon Jacksties
2020

From the Horse's Mouth

From the telling of Hugh Lupton, storyteller, poet, author, teacher

There was once a king who was as kind as he was wise and as wise as he was kind. His sons and his people loved him.

One evening he and his court were feasting when he saw something glimmering on his food. Raising it on the tip of his knife, he held it towards the candle to see it better. The hair shone silver-white in the golden light. Furious, the king ordered that the cook be brought before him. All were silent as they waited for the cook to appear, it was so unusual for their king to display bad temper.

The king sat there, his darkened face fixed on his plate. The hand that held the knife with the silver hair still clinging to the blade, was trembling. The fearful cook came silently into the hall. He stood beside the king, who did not notice him at first until he coughed gently to let him know that he was there. The king looked up, into the face of a young man. The cook had glossy black hair; it would be years before any turned grey. The king had found one of his own hairs on his food. He had grown old without knowing it. 'And they think me wise!' he smiled to himself.

Now that he knew that he was approaching the end of his life, he wondered which of his sons to leave his crown to. All three were clever young men, so he decided to set them a task.

'Bring me the least truthful thing in the land and bring me the most truthful thing in the land.'

The eldest went first. Before long, the king heard the sounds of a struggle outside his chamber. Suddenly the door was kicked open and the eldest prince burst into the room. Under one arm, squirming and protesting, was the prime minister. Under the other arm, protesting and squirming, was the archbishop. The king began to laugh. He laughed and laughed until he could barely speak. At last he managed to gasp,

'Very good, my son, very good, but which is which?' And fell to laughing again.

The middle son went next. He was soon back and placed before his father a portrait and a mirror. The king looked at the image of himself as a young man in his prime. Then he looked at his reflection. He knew he didn't look like his picture any more, but when he looked in the mirror he knew that he didn't feel as old as the old man who stared back at him. He looked from portrait to reflection, from reflection to portrait. Which was true – how he looked or how he felt? Tears ran down his cheeks as he said, 'Very good, my son, very good, but which is which?' And he fell to weeping again.

Then the youngest son set off. He returned when the courtiers were all assembled for the evening meal. There was a gasp when they saw what he held in his hands. It was a horrible sight: in one hand was a withered blackened strip of flesh and in the other was a raw, bleeding, still steaming horse's tongue, fresh from the butcher.

'Do not ask, Father, which is which, for it is easy to tell. In one hand I hold a human tongue that I cut from a corpse hanging on a gibbet. Of all God's creatures, Man is the only one that can lie. Of all of God's creation, the human race is the least truthful. In my other hand is the tongue of a horse, one whom we call a dumb beast. But, oh Father, if we could but understand the language of the birds and the beasts how wise we would be when we listened to those who cannot lie.'

When the youngest son ruled the kingdom, he was wise enough to always have his brothers' company and help at hand.

Wolf and Fox, Enemies of Old

Fox set out on a winter's night
He called on the moon to shine so bright
He'd many a mile to roam that night
Before he reached the farm – o! – farm – o! farm – o!
He'd many a mile to roam that night
Before he reached the farm – o!

On he ran to the farmer's pen
Where ducks and geese were kept therein
'A pair of you will grease my chin
Before I leave this farm – o! farm – o! farm – o!
A pair of you will grease my chin
Before I leave this farm – o!'

Every evening the farmer would drive his oxen home. It didn't matter how hard they had worked during the day, the farmer always complained at how slow they were. Dragging their hooves and stumbling, he never thought that he had driven them too hard. He would sometimes curse them, saying, 'By God, I wish the wolf would eat you!'

Though far away on the hillside, Wolf, with his keen hearing, heard this curse. He wasn't the only one: Fox, always unseen and often too close for comfort, also heard it and much else besides. One hungry night Wolf was waiting by the oxen's pen.

'I have come to claim what is mine.'

'There is nothing of mine that is thine,' said the farmer.

Wolf explained how he had come to collect the oxen that had often been wished to him, and the farmer argued against this. As neither could agree, they decided to take the matter to a judge. At that moment, Fox, who had been secretly listening as usual, materialised out of the dusk and offered to judge the case. The others readily agreed, even though Fox said that in the interests of confidentiality he would have to speak to each of them separately.

The farmer was taken aside first and Fox promised him that he would ensure that Wolf did not take the oxen – for a small fee, of course: 'Just the one goose for myself – oh, and a duck for Vixen.'

The plaintiff was nonplussed for a moment, being used to Fox stealing from him rather than him being put in the position of donor.

'A goose and a duck – small price for a pair of oxen, I think. But if you have a better plan, I quite understand,' said Fox, knowing full well he could always come back later.

Planning was not the man's strong point and he felt more comfortable leaving that to others, even if this meant that a fox was doing his thinking for him. A second bad bargain being struck, Fox trotted off for his confidential interview with Wolf.

'Farmer has reconsidered his hasty words and wants to make you an offer. A pair of oxen is a powerful great mouthful for one wolf. It would take you a month to eat the first and during that time you would have to be providing fodder for the second. It's more trouble than it's worth. Farmer has offered you a whole round of cheese instead.'

Wolf began to drool with hunger, a cheese would be less trouble than butchering an ox. He could think of it as a starter and maybe come back for an ox at a later date, now that he knew where they lived. Fox saw him hesitate: 'If you'll just follow me, I'll show you where the cheese is kept to keep it fresh.'

Fox led Wolf to the well, knowing that the full moon would be reflected in it at exactly that time. Wolf peered into it and saw that a huge round of creamy cheese lay in its depth. A thin strand of drool stretched towards it, breaking the surface of the water. The cheese shivered invitingly, but how to reach it? Fox pointed out the buckets and handle and explained that if they took it in turns to sit in a bucket, their weight would bring them down to the cheese.

'It might be a bit slippery with that water keeping it cool. Could be tricky lifting it – you wouldn't want it to roll away from you like some great wheel,' said Fox. 'Perhaps I should come down and help you with it?'

At that Wolf felt a little wary. Supposing he went down and handed it to Fox, what would prevent him from running off with it – even bowling it before him like the wheel he had mentioned? But if Fox went down first then he would have to pass it to Wolf. Fox was invited to do this and he set off in one of the buckets. Wolf waited till he had reached the bottom before he scrambled into the other bucket. Of course, his descending weight made Fox's bucket rise. As they passed each other Fox said, 'There's always somebody on the way up when there's someone on the way down.'

Wolf stayed at the bottom of the well looking for the cheese until the moon passed over, and Fox collected his promised goose and duck. Not long after that, he collected a few more that had not been promised.

The Black Fox

'Black Fox' is a term given to an animal with a black brush and legs, sometimes a black muzzle or ears too. There have only been a handful of totally black foxes recorded in Britain.

There was once a lord who was the greatest landowner in the region. His estate spanned moor and coombe down to the North coast and the South. Often he would ride his favourite mare, Midnight, up to the highest tor to look in all directions at what was his. To the East and West his land stretched so far that he couldn't see its limits – except for that one little dark patch on the rolling gold of the moor, before the woods dipped down into the coombe behind it. Whenever he saw that his guts twisted inside him because that tiny patch was a little cottage that he didn't own, and couldn't for all his trying.

There that cottage lay, a freehold blot on the landscape of all he possessed. His grandfather had given it outright to its owner, and the deed lay signed and sealed with the county sheriff. It was so long ago that people differed about the story behind that gift. Some said that it was in return for the favour she had done, saving his life after a hunting accident. Some said it was for more favours than that. What was hardest to believe was that the woman, old now beyond reckoning, was still alive – but nobody doubted that Dame Biddy was a healer and had been the best bone setter in the county. Others whispered what they dared not say aloud – that Dame Biddy was a witch. If that rumour had reached him, he didn't wonder at it, as on the few times he had visited her, asking to buy her out for far more than the old cottage was worth, he had spent the following night in agony, gripped by gut-wrenching pains.

One day, the lord rode into town for the market. He noticed a stranger, a haughty young woman with red hair and a sinuous grace about her. He tried to catch her eye, but she slipped around the stalls in such a way that he couldn't get close enough. Whenever he caught a glimpse of her and set off in her direction, she was gone, only to appear suddenly elsewhere. However, he soon forgot about her when a servant rushed up to him and whispered the news that Dame Biddy had died.

The next day he galloped over to the cottage, but reined Midnight in with a savagery she never deserved. There was smoke rising from the chimney. When he rode closer he could see washing on the line – two pairs of black stockings and a russet cloak. There came a sudden gust and the cloak fought it, turning itself almost inside out, revealing its black lining and startling the mare. As she bolted, he seemed to hear harsh, sawing laughter coming from the cottage. Somehow that mocking bark of a laugh deterred him from calling in person. It was his servant who told him that Dame Biddy had left the cottage to her great niece – and once more there was nothing he could do about getting it for himself.

It was strange, in those distant days, for a young woman to be living by herself. Many admired or even envied her independent ways. Footloose and fancy free she seemed, with a flashing grin for those she passed on her jaunts. She trotted along the lanes on fast, silent feet, her red hair sleek and glossy and her bright eyes sliding into that quick sly smile, so that none could have said what colour they were.

Everyone knew that she didn't work but no one knew what she lived on. From time to time she would pass the lord in a narrow lane and it irked him that she had eyes only for his horse and not for him. It took a while for him to realise that it was she who had moved into what should have been his property.

He hated her for this, but could not admit how much he was attracted to her. Unable to stay away at last, he visited on the pretext of offering her work at the big house. He found her in the garden. Her only answer was to bark that harsh laugh at him, her crimson mouth drawn back over pointed white teeth. Then she ran, leaping the garden wall to get away.

So the lord resorted to his one pleasure, that of hunting, the only thing that he had shared with his grandfather. Although he kept the best pack of hounds in the county, he would sometimes be invited to join other hunts. These were the only occasions when he would meet his neighbours, landowners like himself but none as wealthy. That season they were all talking about the highway robberies that were taking place on the moor, and of a highwayman who seemed to know exactly where and when the coaches would be passing even though routes and times had been varied.

The lord was more troubled by his mount, so unusually listless. Midnight, always ahead in the field, had hung back and barely cleared a gate. When he returned home he questioned the grooms. One admitted to finding her in a sweat first thing, even though she had been thoroughly groomed the night before. The grooms took it in turn to watch through the night from the hayloft. They never saw anything, although some mornings still found Midnight sweating and restless though tired. Fearing their master's anger, they never mentioned these occasions, and rubbed her down so that her coat was as glossy as it should be. One of the cleverer grooms took some long hairs from her tail and attached them lightly to her tack, but on those troubled mornings, they were found to still be in place.

When the hunting season was over, the lord had nothing to distract himself from thinking of that cunning young woman he so hated to be fancying. Then the solution occurred to him: he would marry her. She would be his and as everything belonged to the husband after marriage, the cottage would also be his at last. He didn't notice how Midnight's head drooped and how she stumbled as he rode to that lonely dwelling. He was in the cottage and as the door swung behind him, the offer was out of his mouth. Even he could see how agitated the woman was and he laid a hand on her arm. She bit, hard. Unbelieving, he heard bone crunch before he tore his hand from her mouth. Then she was gone, slipped past him. Rage burned fiercer than his wounded hand.

That night there was a fire. Nobody knew how it started, or if they did they weren't saying. That cottage burned down stock and stone. Nobody was sure what those black greasy remains had once been. Silently they watched the lord poking them with his ebony cane. If anyone noticed a sprinkle of sharp white teeth amongst them, nobody said.

On the first day of the new hunting season a large black fox was sighted. All day the lord's hounds chased it, without seeming to get any nearer. It was started by the next hunt and the next, but the pack never seemed any closer to making a kill. Before any other fox could be sighted, the same black fox always appeared. Some said the brush was too slender for a fox's – this had to be a vixen. Some said that no vixen was ever that large, that this animal was bigger than most dog foxes. The season wore on and that fox grew bolder and bolder. It would lead the pack on through boggy land where some were lost even though their quarry skimmed along that treacherous ground unharmed. The lord would whip hounds and horses beyond endurance and some were lost or injured that way too. Still he hunted on through the season with only half a pack, determined that however few remained would tear that beast apart before his eyes.

On the last hunt of the season, the black fox made sure its scent led to the stone wall that surrounded the garden of the burned cottage. Hiding behind the wall, it waited until the lord rode up. Then with one leap it was on top of the wall and at eye level with its hunter. A sly look, a flashing grin and Midnight reared, throwing her rider. This time there was no Dame Biddy to set his bones. The lord never regained his senses, but it was clear from his fevered cries and mutterings that in his mind he was still hunting the black fox until the day he died.

Hare Here on Earth

This tale has been inspired by a recording from Giles Abbott, storyteller, who was told it by a lady from the gypsy community. It is written here with Giles' kind permission.

Long ago, when Time was new, all things were alive and all creatures spoke to each other. Sun and Moon, those most glorious of beings, showed their celestial love by creating a daughter. Hare leaped and bounded across the heavens, zigzagging her way between one parent and the other. Every time one of her paws touched the sky, a star appeared. Time smiled to see how her increase was measured across the sky in countless silver tracks.

Sun and Moon smiled to see how strong and fast their daughter had become, how tireless and nimble. Hare had reached her full strength. One day – or was it night? – she looked down and noticed Earth for the first time. Earth felt her gaze and looked upwards at the delicate paths of silver that followed this magical creature as she danced about. The moment when Earth noticed Hare, was the moment they fell in love.

24

Hare bounded off to tell her parents the wonderful news that she had found a lover, and one, moreover, who requited her feelings. Sun and Moon asked who she was considering uniting herself with, and Hare proudly told them that it was Earth. Her parents were appalled. How could their celestial daughter decide to have anything to do with a creature so base, so dense, who was incapable of producing any light? They told her that they would never have anything to do with her choice, and that if she persisted, they would not bless this shameful liaison.

But Hare was in love and hurt that her parents' love for her did not exceed their misplaced pride. She decided to leave the sky forever and live with her lover. From that day – or was it night? – to this, she has stayed on Earth. She became the totem animal of love and fertility, and was venerated as the Goddess Oestra. She gave her name to our spring festival of Easter, and the female hormone oestrogen. Trusting that her consort will protect their children, she doesn't make a home or burrow for them, but leaves them pressed close against the ground. During the spring equinox her children dance upright to give Sun and Moon an equal chance to see their grandchildren.

The Hare and the Black Dog

From the fifteenth to the seventeenth century, most people in Britain believed in the widespread practice of witchcraft or, if they didn't, were wise enough to remain silent. Many hundreds were burned or hanged for this 'crime'. It was believed that their magical powers enabled them to take on the form of an animal, often that of a hare. As the vast majority convicted of witchcraft were women, it is not surprising that they were associated with an animal that was revered as a manifestation of the goddess of fertility in the old religion. Queen Boudicca of the Iceni tribe in East Anglia would release two hares from her robes as a gift to the Goddess and a source of divination before a battle. It was in East Anglia where most of the witchcraft trials and death sentences occurred.

An example of this kind of trial can be seen in that of the conviction and hanging of a woman, unusually named Julian Cox, in 1663. The testimony of a huntsman, amongst others, was enough to convict her. He had started a hare that, after a long chase, took refuge in a bush. When he went around it, he found an old woman on all fours who was too out of breath to speak. It was obvious to him (and everyone else) that she had been the hare he had been hunting.

Folk tales hardly differ from what was deemed sufficient evidence to bring about a death sentence, as in the following tale.

Some men were out hunting hare one day, but they hadn't much luck. As they roamed about with their dogs, they came across an old woman who was well known for being a witch, although none had dared accuse her openly. Half in jest they asked her if she had seen any hares thereabouts, it being well known that witches like to transform into hares, often taunting huntsmen by leading them on a merry and futile chase.

She told them that they might catch their hare if they searched in a particular direction, as long as they didn't permit a black dog to join their pack. As none of them had a black dog there was little danger of this happening, and they set off in the direction that she had indicated, thinking that they had nothing to lose by so doing. To their surprise they started a large hare, who gave men and dogs such a run for their money they feared they would lose her. But the dogs picked up her trail again and all gave chase as she doubled back towards the old woman's hovel. Then, clearing a hedge with one bound, a large black dog appeared that nobody recognised.

'It were as big as Black Shuck himself,' claimed the men as they related the tale in the inn afterwards.

Maybe it was indeed this phantom dog, creature of ill omen that terrified night travellers, or maybe it was a stray, but it seized the hare by her hind leg. She raked its eyes with her claws and managed to struggle free, seeming to make straight for the back of the old woman's home. Some of the braver amongst the party entered to investigate and found the old woman staunching a bleeding wound in her leg.

Deer Dreaming

Some girls were gathering blueberries on the slopes of the mountain. They climbed higher as that was where the juiciest were to be found. Suddenly a wall of mist came down and one of them became separated from her companions. Thicker and thicker grew the mist. Her calls were muffled by its grey blanket and the sunlight was blotted out. Soon she realised that she was quite lost and feared to walk in any direction in case she fell over a cliff. If that were not bad enough, she saw huge dark shapes looming towards her. Rooted with fear, she didn't know if she was surrounded by ogres or trolls. One was now so close that she could see the shape of horns, black against the grey. Was it some fearsome mountain spirit, or even the Devil himself?

There came a sudden gust of wind that blew the mist away and she could see that the shapes were a herd of deer, the horns those of the stag who guarded them. The animals took no notice of her, not even the stag, and instead of being fearful, she began to feel relief. Surprised to find deer foraging so high on the mountain, she saw that they were grazing on a moss that grew amongst the rocks. Surely these animals knew their way about the mountains and as they seemed to tolerate her, perhaps, if she stayed amongst them, they would eventually lead her to safety? They grazed on contentedly and the girl felt calm in their company.

Suddenly they all raised their heads and looked towards a certain direction, as though responding to a sound that she couldn't hear. Then the herd set off towards it. As they were moving slowly due to their fawns, it was easy for her to keep up. Indeed, it seemed that if she stumbled or lagged behind, they paused for her to catch up.

At last they reached a huge cavern that led into the mountainside. There she saw an ancient couple gazing into a dark pool in the cave's floor. Old Woman arose and went to fetch a wooden milking pail, with which she started to milk the hinds. The girl asked if she could have shelter with them for the night and Old Woman went to speak with Old Man in a language that she could not understand. She was told that it would not be possible to give her shelter for only one night; however, she could stay with them for a year and a day if she helped them with the work of the dairy.

'We are getting old and we would welcome your help,' said Old Woman, who seemed to be as ancient as the mountain itself.

Being utterly lost and knowing that she would perish on the mountainside without shelter, the girl, seeing that she had little choice, agreed.

She worked hard for the old couple. One of her duties was to forage on the slopes and gather thyme, bog myrtle, meadowsweet, mint and golden asphodel. She helped Old Woman to dry these and spread them on the heather that burned beneath the pot in which she was making crowdie* from the hinds' milk.

* *Crowdie is a soft and therefore malleable cheese, a staple food in the Highlands.*

'This is my life's work you are helping with,' said Old Woman.

Meanwhile, Old Man would gaze into the dark pool on the cave's floor, which was a mirror for all the world. He would then take his wife's crowdie and shape it into the figures that he had seen in the pool. At sunset, he would hold these up so that they took on the colours from the sun's rays in all their variety of hues. These figures were to become dreams. It was Old Man's life work to fashion these, and together the couple were the makers of all the dreams in the world.

When the crowdie figures had taken their colours from the setting sun, Old Man would hold some of them up in his right hand. These were the true dreams for those who were beloved. From out of the blue heavens came birds of good omen: eagles, falcons, larks and wrens. It was the task of these birds to carry these dreams throughout the world. The dreams that Old Man held up in his left hand were those of false, misleading phantoms. From out of the dark sky came birds of ill omen: ravens, hoodies and kites, smelling of carrion. It was their task to spread evil and deceiving dreams throughout the world.

When a year and a day had passed. Old Woman thanked the girl for all she had done. As she had worked so hard for them, she was to be well rewarded, and was told to be guided by the deer. The sun had set, but nevertheless, she left the cave and walked amongst the hinds and fawns, the stag taking up the rear. All through the night they walked, stepping surely amongst the rocks as though it were day. In the grey light of dawn they led her down to a strange shore, onto a beach she had never seen before. She tried to walk along it, but her escort would not allow her, bunching around her to keep her standing in their midst. Then the deer all gazed out to sea with that same concentration she had observed during her first encounter.

Silhouetted against the sunrise, the girl could make out a small dark shape on the sea. The shape was getting larger because it was getting nearer. Soon she could make out a small boat with a single sailor. The craft, made of skins, beached, and a young man leaped out. Slowly he came towards her, then he held out his arms.

'Fair One of Dreams, I have found you at last. I knew I would never rest until I could show my father, the King, that my dream was as true as water is wet. When I dreamed of you, my search began.' Then he kneeled before her in the sand.

'It was also in my dream that when I proposed to you, you were about to accept me, but I awoke before I could hear your beloved voice say...'

'Yes!' said Young Woman.

The deer watched as she climbed into the boat with her prince, who rowed them both back across the sea. In time Young Woman became queen in her new country. She had a particular skill for interpreting dreams, and many came to tell her theirs, which is why there came to be many wise people in that land.

Deer Wife, Deer Son

Finn Mac Cumhaill, the greatest warrior that Ireland had ever known, now rarely left his own fort. His loyal companions, the Fianna, the most skilled warriors on the whole island, were restless now that their leader no longer summoned them to the adventures for which they were famous. And if that was not bad enough, it was a long time since their hunting horns had sounded through the woods that stretched across the land from one coast to the other.

Finn had never recovered from the loss of his beloved Sabha, the fairy woman he had found in the forest. Many times in the day he recalled how they had first met, his hounds eager with the scents of the first hunts of autumn. It was the day before Samhain, the day we now call Halloween, when the ways between this world and the Other World are open.

He and his companions had been hunting together, when their hounds flushed a quarry. There was a streak of warm brown bounding through the trees, and the dogs, unleashed, tried to turn it towards open country. The men ran after the pack, spears and bows at the ready. They had cleared the treeline, but a sudden rise hid the pack from view. Finn was leading his band when he heard the last sound he would ever expect to hear on a hunt – there was a growling and a snarling as the pack turned on itself. A dog fight was about to break out. He breasted the slope just in time. There were his own hounds, Bran and Sceolan, standing guard in front of a doe, keeping the rest of the pack at bay. Hackles raised, teeth bared in threat, their growls promised death to any dog that came nearer.

The trembling doe was backed up against a jumble of rocks. Her shining dark eyes stared into Finn's and held his gaze. He felt a tingling in the thumb that had been splashed by a magical potion in his youth. Whenever he felt that sensation it meant that he was in the presence of magic, or that beings from the Other World were close. Bran and Sceolan had lived in that other place too, and had recognised what Finn now knew. He and his companions called off the pack and Bran and Sceolan came to heel, their tales wagging.

Everyone watched as the doe slowly walked towards her rescuer. She deliberately brushed him as she passed, delicately stepped a little further on before pausing. Then she looked back at him before continuing her escape, not back to the woods, but towards his home. She soon stopped again, and again looked back at Finn. It was clear that she meant him to follow her. Bran and Sceolan were now flanking her like a guard of honour, the Fianna and the rest of the pack following at a distance.

What a sight met those who had remained at the fort. A beautiful doe, escorted by two proud hounds with Finn striding behind them, his arrows in their quiver, his spear slung at his back. Bringing up the rear was the rest of the hunting band, their deer hounds on the leash.

When she reached the palisade of the fort, she stopped at the entrance. Then she stepped over the threshold, but did not clear it. The day had darkened towards dusk, so at first everyone could tell themselves that it was a trick of the light that deceived their eyes.

Legs straddling, her body began to shiver. The coppery glint of her skin shimmered in the last of the light. Her shape retracted, her head shrinking back towards her body, dragging her forelegs with it. Standing only on her hind legs, her body drew itself upwards. She stood there, chrysalis shaped, looming in the gathering dark. Then so sweet a music was heard that it squeezed tears out of the eyes of the most hardened warriors. With that music came the scent of bluebell woods, the soughing of the wind in mighty oak trees, the warm caress of spring sunshine. Then there was a tearing sound as the deer skin split from top to toe. Out of it stepped Sabha, the fairy woman.

In the amazed silence, Bran and Sceolan measured their height with hers, placed eager paws on her shoulders, joyful in their remembering. Her fall of copper hair hid tears of relief before those loyal hounds could lick them away in greeting. Now that her long enchantment was over, she turned to her human rescuer and waited for him to invite her into his home.

The Fianna soon heard the story of Sabha's double escape – from her world and her enchantment. A magician amongst the fairy folk had long wanted her for his own. She feared and disliked him and always refused his advances. Nevertheless, he pursued her and she spent most of her life avoiding him. At last she was to see how well she had judged him. Realising that he would never prevail, he shaped his anger into a spell:

Lovely as the delicate doe,
You have fled from me at every sound of my step.
I have hunted you with words sweet as the scent of bluebells, I have
hunted you with promises strong as the oak,
I have hunted you with longing, hopeful as each dawn.
I have hunted you with desire flaming as any sunset
And still you have hidden from me.
If I cannot have you, then no man will ever have you
Unless that having brings you your death.
Beautiful and fearful as you are,
I will shift your shape into that of a deer.
Let any man hunt you at their will.
Let this enchantment lie upon you until the day
A man you do not fear stays his hand from his quiver,
Stays his hand from his shaft,
Sending neither arrow nor spear against you.

She had fallen on her knees begging him not to curse her in this way, but he had touched her with his wand of yew. There on all fours, she had seen her arms stretch into slender legs. Still she pleaded with him as soft hands turned into hard hooves. Hearing her voice distort as her jaws lengthened, her widening eyes took in his mockery as she fell silent forever.

Hidden in the woods of Fairyland she would shadow her own kind without being seen – King Finvarra of the Fair Folk loved hunting too. She would listen to the tales her people told, most carefully to the ones of visitors from another world. She remembered her pity when these mortals had been transformed into fairy hounds and of how she had always been kind to them, feeding them titbits during the great feasts. She heard the tale of how they had been gifted to a great hero – though some said they had been stolen – and of how that hero had a magical thumb that gave him more than mortal powers.

She noted well the stories of Finn's adventures and at last she learned where he and his companions gathered. She waited for the time when the gates between the worlds were open, tried to get as close as possible to his fort, fought the fear that made her animal self want to flee.

Sabha was Finn's guest and under his protection. She had escaped from a man who had hunted her whilst in her true form and cursed her to be hunted by all others in her enchanted form. So it was that Finn, the honourable host, the honourable man, hid his own love for her. But his days were filled with the sight of her hair glowing like autumn sun through the beech trees, and his nights were filled with the sight of her flame-rich hair in the firelight. There came a night when it was Sabha who went to where Finn lay in a waking dream, turning it into one that he could touch, one that did not fade in the following days and nights.

At first the Fianna were happy for their captain, but as the days passed into weeks and months they grew restless. Finn had eyes and ears only for Sabha. It was a though he lay under a love spell stronger than any mortal woman could cast. Without their leader there were no more noble deeds or adventures and mutterings of discontent were heard. To what avail their oaths of loyalty to the most revered band in Ireland? It was as if the mighty Fianna were no more.

A day came when Viking raiders were seen off the coast, marauders searching for the most valuable cargo of all – that of human slaves. At last Finn roused himself at this threat and the war band was prepared. Fearful of leaving Sabha unprotected, he made her promise not to leave the fort until his return – a promise easily given.

The Fianna, with Finn leading them as of old, easily repelled the attack, and it was not long before they were home. But it was a silent place that Finn returned to. There were no servants to be seen. His calls for Sabha were not answered. At last when he found his steward, he heard the tale he was already dreading.

Every evening since the band had left, Sabha would go to the palisade and climb up to the top of the closed gates, looking for the heroes' return. The steward always accompanied her. The previous evening was the same as the others until they saw Finn's unmistakable silhouette. As he approached, they clearly saw master and lover. He waved and beckoned. Without even waiting for the steward to open the gates, Sabha had climbed over, and, supple as a cat, she had slipped down the other side and was running towards Finn. As soon as she was outside the fort's shadow she stopped. There was no hurried embrace that the onlooker on the palisade had been expecting. Instead a shimmer passed over the man, a ripple of light swept him from top to toe and then the shape-shifting stranger no more resembled Finn than would a king a beggar.

It was clear to the steward that this was no stranger to the woman as she hid her face from him. Her cries of 'No, not you, not you again!' turned to the whimpers an animal makes in a trap. As he ran towards his mistress, that fearsome stranger raised his arm and pointed. What in Finn's hand would have been a sword, was now a wand of yew. The steward felt his blood slow, his breath fade, his limbs weighty as stone. Helpless, unable to move, he could only watch. The wand struck Sabha and her body shimmered, shifted. Her woman shape crumpled to one on all fours. Her copper hair clothed her as a hide. Trembling ears pointed, huge dark eyes spilled over as she looked at Finn's dwelling for a last time. The stranger had turned, was walking towards the darkening horizon. Stiff legged, compelled, she followed.

From that day Finn was not the same. He fulfilled his duties as leader but only to the minimum extent. He no longer went on a quest for the thrill of an adventure. There was no joy in him for play or laughter. Every spare moment was spent in combing the woods with Bran and Sceolan, calling Sabha's name with only Echo's sad reply. He banned hunting in the forest. This was one of the hardest things for the Fianna to bear. Now the only game they ate was boar meat when the wild pigs came to rob the crops. The deer flourished. Because they multiplied, so did the wolves. Sometimes flocks were attacked. The forest could not keep growing at the same pace as the deer herds. It was being eaten away from the new shoots down to the bark. The forest itself was dying.

At last the Fianna persuaded Finn to lift the ban on hunting.

'If the forest dies, the people will say that the land is dying. Have you not sworn to be protector of the land of Ireland?'

So it was that one Samhain, seven years after finding Sabha, Finn found himself hunting again. His heart was not in it – let his eager band flush a quarry, make a kill. His mind wandered as it always did when he saw those beech leaves in autumn. But then he heard an unexpected noise – a growling and a snarling as the pack turned on itself. A dog fight was about to break out. His ears heard it, but the sound spoke louder to his memory. He rushed towards it. Hope pulsed through him stronger than blood.

When he reached the pack, Bran and Sceolan were backed up against a thicket, holding the rest at bay. There was no sign of doe or woman. Sabha was not there. A rustling came from the thicket, low to the ground. Finn raised his spear. Sceolan's warning growl deepened, Bran was ready to spring at his master. A lesser man would have slain his hound at that moment, but Finn, despite his surprise, felt a tingling in his thumb. He lowered his spear. Bran and Sceolan sprang aside for him as he thrust an arm into the bush and pulled out a biting, scratching, naked child. Thin and filthy, spitting and snarling, it was more wild animal than human.

People had heard of wild children raised in the woods by wolves. Perhaps this was one. He was taken back to the fort, where at first he would only sleep curled up with Finn's hounds. When he stroked them, his huge dark eyes would brim with tears. Strangely he would not at first eat meat, only fruits, nuts and sometimes bread. In time he learned to speak.

He told Finn that his mother was a deer and that they lived in a wooded valley where it was always summer. A man would come and ugly sounds came from his mouth. When this happened, his mother would tremble with fear and try to hide. She was never able to get away from him and then the ugly sounds would get louder. The boy hated the man. When he was older and the man came again, the child had attacked him, biting and scratching. The man's face had grown dark and huge, until the boy could not tell whether he was looking up at his face or the sky. His mouth had grown louder and he could not tell if it had become thunder. There had been a flash and he had found himself in another part of the forest, or in another forest where it was cold and the leaves were the wrong colour. Starving and lost, he had looked for his mother for a long time before Bran and Sceolan had found him.

Finn wept as he listened – but none knew whether it was for the loss of his lover or for the joy that followed sorrow in the finding of his son.

'I will call you Oisin in memory of your mother.'

That is how Finn first knew his own son when he was seven years old and gave him a name that means 'Little Fawn' in Irish. This child, although never having heard human speech before he was half grown, became the greatest poet that Ireland has ever known. It is believed that it was Oisin who first gave us the story of how his father found his mother and eventually himself.

King Arthur and the Ermine Cloak

The pelt of the ermine has been a sought-after status symbol for centuries. To this day, on ceremonial occasions, the aristocracy and members of elite office such as judges, wear robes made of many ermine skins. The number of pelts and the distribution of the dark marks made by the tips of the tails constitute a code, rigorously upheld by traditional practice, that indicates where the wearer is placed in the aristocratic hierarchy.

Pre-Christian stories tell that if an ermine accidentally sullied its coat with mud, it would swoon with horror. In this scientifically aware age, it is hard to credit that an animal may have a reaction more suited to the supermodels of today! However, this belief informed hunting practices into medieval times. Ermine would be prevented from retreating into their burrows by placing a barrier of mud around them. Rather than dirtying their coats, it was thought that they would surrender to their hunters as death was more desirable than dirt. This belief gave rise to mottos such as 'Death before Defilement', which are sometimes depicted along with heraldic imagery derived from that revered coat.

The stoat, a small brown voracious predator, only has a pale patch on its throat and belly during much of the year. Its winter transformation into an ermine, with its pure white coat, seems a miraculous alteration. This change was revered as a symbol of transcendence from the earthly to the spiritual. Painters of religious subjects dressed personages of holy status in ermine, at a time when worshippers understood this symbol to denote spiritual purity.

King Arthur's links with Gaul and Brittany were strong, but he lost lands in Gaul and returned to Britain. Meanwhile, a cruel and despotic ruler oppressed the people of Brittany, and had a particular hatred of Christians. He would destroy their shrines and delighted in blaspheming against the Virgin Mary, knowing that this would cause the most offence. Word of this had reached Arthur, and one day at court, a knight publicly mocked him for doing nothing about it. It was time to act.

He swore that he would avenge the insults to the Virgin Mary, gathered an army, and returned to Brittany. The miscreant Flolo challenged Arthur to choose a champion to fight him. Although many of his knights offered, because of his vow, Arthur would not let anyone fight in his stead. It was decided that the site of their battle would be on the Île de la Cité on the River Seine. However, Flolo was a giant and even though Arthur fought valiantly, his enemy managed to give him such a blow that he fell fainting to his knees. It was his knights who later told him that just as the giant was about to swipe off his head, the Virgin Mary herself appeared. She swept off her ermine cloak and draped it across Arthur's shield. Its pure white brilliance dazzled Flolo, who raised his own shield to hide his eyes from the blinding glory of the cloak. This gave Arthur the few moments he needed to recover. He ducked beneath the giant's guard and it was his legendary sword, Excalibur, that delivered a death blow to the giant instead.

To give thanks for his safety, and to make amends for the Christian sites that had been desecrated, King Arthur decreed that a church be built on the site of his deliverance. He ordered it to be dedicated to Our Lady. From that day to this, the heraldic shield for Brittany has been a field of ermine. True to Arthur's promise, the cathedral of Notre Dame stands to this day on the Île de la Cité in Paris, surviving the fire that threatened to destroy it only a few days before the author rewrote this legend in 2019.

How Ferret Came to Be

Although only two rats had been admitted onto the Ark, they soon set about making up for this deficit. Maybe Mrs Rat had already been 'expecting' when taken aboard, but before long, and as with many boats, there were more rats than was comfortable. Noah sent word to his son, Shem, to get rid of them. Shem wasn't sure how and asked his brother Ham, who told him that the problem was already being dealt with.

Apparently two female polecats had cunningly avoided their mates so that they could get onto the Ark instead of them. Noah had been too busy to notice that there hadn't been one of each gender. Two male stoats, never known for their good manners, had perpetrated the same ruse. Romances are said to blossom on sea voyages. The stoats and polecats found each other irresistible and their unions had resulted in the birth of the first ever ferrets. These creatures, hitherto unknown to God or man, were busy dispatching the rats. (At least two of these must have escaped to plague future shipping.)

The discerning reader will wonder how it is that polecats and stoats have survived to this day. The only explanation can be that other genders of these sinuous creatures, reputed to be able to get into the smallest of spaces, survived as stowaways.

The Grateful Weasel

A man set off to tend his potato fields in a part of the townland that was at some distance from his home. The weather being fine, he took off his boots, knotted the laces together and slung them around his neck. This was common practice to save the leather in the days when any repairs had to await the unpredictable return of the travelling cobblers.

On reaching his land, he donned his boots once more to protect his feet against clods and tools whilst working. The journey home saw them hanging around his neck once more.

Hearing a dreadful noise of squeaking and squealing, he paused at his neighbour's garden wall to see what was making those sounds of desperate anguish.

There he saw a rat and a weasel locked in mortal combat. As more wounds appeared, their battle cries increased and he watched, fascinated, as to the outcome. He even wondered as to which creature he would be laying his money on, were he a betting man. Perhaps it was a person's natural empathy for the underdog, or the memory of how much of his produce had been lost to rats when, seeing that the rat was gaining the upper hand, he began to fear for the weasel. Then the rat caught weasel in a stranglehold, and he could not refrain from action.

It being a life or death situation, there was no time for him to untie and put on his boots. He leaped over his neighbour's wall, and held the rat down with his foot. The vermin, faced with a larger adversary, promptly turned his head and bit deep into his toe. This allowed the weasel, with a final twist of her agile body, to make her escape, bloodied but alive.

Later that day, whilst working in a closer field, the man's foot began to throb with pain. Even the leg seemed swollen and discoloured. How could the contamination from the rat's teeth be working so quickly? He tried to hobble home, but within moments was in such pain that he could no longer put any weight on that foot. Sinking to the ground, his cries for help brought the neighbours, who carried him back to his kitchen. There the boot had to be cut from his foot. Purple and swollen, his big toe was as large as his heel and the foot itself had become a shapeless bulge.

With no physicians near, the good women of the village did what they could with poultices and applications of hot or cold flannels and hot or cold poteen. Nothing helped, and by now the man was in a raging fever as the poison from the rat's fangs spread throughout his body. The villagers were now thinking in terms of a priest rather than a doctor. There was no more they could do except wait and see which way Nature's course would run.

The back door had been left open so that his neighbour could hear him call if she was needed. The invalid had been made as comfortable as possible by the kitchen fire, his poisoned leg stretched out before him – although his helpers couldn't be sure whether he was even aware of these ministrations. As he sat there, helpless, he saw a streak of ginger as the weasel entered the kitchen. Without hesitating, she approached him and tenderly laid a piece of greenery on his afflicted toe. Perhaps he dozed off, but there she was again, now with a different herb between her jaws, which she laid beside the first. She returned a third time with yet another kind of plant, leaving it alongside the others.

Then he fell into a deep and healing sleep. When he awoke his foot had returned to normal, apart from two tiny red puncture wounds where he had been bitten. Were it not for these and the now withering herbs that had dropped to the floor, he would have thought it all a dream. He gathered up the plants and buried them in the garden under the spot where the weasel's rescue had taken place. When his astonished neighbours saw him doing this, he told them what had happened. Since then, no man, woman or child has harmed a weasel in that place and it became known as Bhaile na Easog, 'The Village of the Weasel'.

St Columba and the Squirrel

St Columba was feeling dispirited. He had spent long years converting, or trying to convert, the pagans in Scotland. But now he was wondering whether he had had any lasting effect, so given were people to falling into their old ways. Heavy of heart, he decided to leave Iona and retreat into Nature until his true path could be revealed to him. Living like a hermit, he found peace amongst the wild places, where he prayed to God to give him a sign.

Wandering through the forest, with ever a prayer on his lips, he came across a clearing. There a glimmer of light caught his eye and he was astonished to see a squirrel dipping her tail in a pool of water and then flicking it onto the moss beside the pool. The sprinkling gesture and the brightness of the water reminded him of something, but so long had he been in the wilderness that it took him a while before he realised that the motions were as those in the rite of baptism.

He continued to watch and realised that she was trying to empty the pool with her beautiful fluffy tail, soaking up the water and violently shaking out the moisture over the ground. Watching her huge efforts, he felt sorry for the little beast.

'Little Squirrel, I don't know why you seek to empty this pool, but the pool is large and however hard you work, your lifespan will not be long enough to see you succeed at this task.'

The squirrel stopped just as though she had understood him. He gathered some nuts and gently laid them beside the little beast. As he turned to leave, he heard the squirrel say, 'Thank you for your kindness, Holy Man. You are right in what you say. I have sought to empty this pool because beneath it lies a bitter soil which makes its waters unsafe to drink. Many animals have suffered from it. I will die long before it has been emptied, but I am making the task easier for those who follow me.'

So saying, she resumed her task. St Columba was inspired by her example. With the realisation that, through the ages, others would carry on the work he had started, and with renewed faith in his mission, he returned to preaching. Whenever he felt dispirited again, he saw in his mind's eye that vivid little creature and the sparkling drops that spoke of her selfless dedication.

Bear Skin

There was once a king who had an only daughter on whom he doted. He was so worried that something would happen to her that he never allowed her to leave the palace and she was followed everywhere by her nurse. When she grew older she realised that she was a prisoner in her own home, and longed to see the outside world. At last she burst out in a passion to her nurse, 'Whilst you were always kind to me when I was a child, now you are my gaoler, sent to spy on me by my father!'

The nurse replied that she loved her as dearly as her father did, but she could see that the time had now come for the princess to be allowed her freedom. She reminded the young woman that her father would give her anything she asked for as long as it wasn't to go outside the palace grounds. She then told her to ask for a wooden wheelbarrow and a bear's skin. The princess was as surprised at this as was the king, but she did as her nurse suggested. Her father thought that she wanted to play at gardening and at dressing up, not having noticed that his darling daughter was no longer a child.

When she returned with the wheelbarrow and the bear skin, she found the nurse waiting with her darning needle. As the princess watched, the needle became longer and thicker until she could see that the nurse was holding a twisted stick in her hand. This was the first moment she realised that apart from being a nurse, the woman was also a sorceress and that what she was holding was a magic wand made of hawthorn. She touched the wheelbarrow with the wand and it began to move of its own accord. Then she told the princess to put on the bear skin and with one touch of the wand, it clung to her as though it were the only skin her body had ever known. No one could have known that standing before them was really a human, not a bear. The sorceress explained that the wheelbarrow would take her wherever she wanted, commanded by the hawthorn wand, and that nobody would be able to penetrate her disguise.

Delighted, the bear princess seated herself in the wheelbarrow and shot off through the palace gates, into the forest. If any of the servants saw her, they didn't believe their eyes, so her escape went unimpeded. Full of wonder at this wild world that had been denied her, she touched the wheelbarrow with the wand to stop it so that she could dismount and examine a wild rose bush. Whilst this was happening, a prince who was out hunting came upon her and surrounded her with his hounds. At that moment she became more outraged princess than fearful bear, 'How dare you set your dogs upon me, who has never done you any harm? Call them off instantly!'

The prince was astonished to come upon a talking bear and did not want to harm it. He called off the dogs and asked the bear whether it would like to accompany him to his own palace, where his parents and courtiers would delight in meeting a bear that could speak. The bear princess was happy to take up this invitation as she was as curious about other palaces as she was about the rest of the world. She leaped into the wheelbarrow and followed the prince. If he was astonished at this mode of transport, he didn't say so as it was no less strange than a bear that could talk.

When she reached the prince's palace she was, of course, a marvel and the centre of attention. As she was used to this, she took it in her stride and thought nothing of it. Everyone adored her and she even won round the servants as she helped them with their chores, which, surprisingly as a princess, she knew how to do. This was because, with no playmates and being confined to her home, she had helped her servants with their work rather than succumb to boredom.

Time passed and she was no longer a novelty. If anything, she was rather being taken for granted, but this was better than being a prisoner in her own palace, and she could run off into the forest whenever she wanted, which was often. The main reason why she stayed, however, was that she had fallen in love with the prince and didn't know what to do about it.

One day, lying under the table, as was her habit, she heard the family discussing a ball that was being held in a kingdom on the other side of the forest. She rolled out from under the table and asked to be taken too. The prince was outraged at this request – the very idea of a bear at a ball! He grabbed her by the scruff of her neck, kicked her up the backside and out of the room.

When he had set off for the party, the bear begged the queen to be allowed to follow him. Taking pity on her protégè, the queen agreed, as long as the bear promised to look from a distance and did not attempt to dance.

'As I am a bear, dear Queen, I promise.'

The bear went to the wheelbarrow and touched it with the wand. It became a fine carriage drawn by a team of four grey mares. Inside it appeared an exquisite dress made of moonbeams. The bear touched her fur with the wand, which shrank away from her human form. She was then able to put on the moonbeam dress and ride off to the ball with the bear skin as her travelling rug.

The prince was enchanted by this beautiful and exotic stranger and would dance with no one else. From the first handclasp he was hopelessly in love. Towards the end of the ball, the bear princess knew that she would have to get home before him. She managed to slip away, hurled herself into her carriage and was off. The prince dashed after the carriage, but a great mist came down and he couldn't see where it had gone. Hidden by the mist, the bear princess touched her carriage with the wand and it became the wheelbarrow once more. The moonbeam dress disappeared and she put on her bear skin. The bear was safely back under the table by the time the prince, delayed by the mist, returned to tell his mother about his new love. They ignored the deep sighs that came from their furry companion as she too heard the tale.

Royal balls in those times lasted for several nights. On the second night, the prince left in a great hurry to be there early in case the love of his life appeared again. Without saying anything to anyone, the bear did just as she had done before. This time her equipage was of chestnut stallions and her dress was made from sunbeams. How she dazzled! How people wondered where this goddess in human form had sprung from! All night the prince was dizzy with delight, but just as he tried to ask her who she was, she slipped from his arms and was gone. This time he had his charger prepared and waiting and was able to gallop after her. However, a furious storm broke out of nowhere and a streak of lightning caused his mount to bolt. By the time he returned home, the bear was under the table and nobody knew she had ever left. He confided his concerns to his mother of never being able to find out who his love was or where she lived. If anything, the noises from the bear sounded like laughter, and the prince gave the animal a good kick for her lack of sympathy.

On the third night, the bear princess appeared in a carriage drawn by dapple greys and her dress was made of starlight. This time the prince slid a ring onto her finger as the ball drew to an end. The prince managed to pursue her nearly as far as the forest but was finally driven back by a mighty wind that blew up from nowhere. Before she touched the magic wand to her body, the princess carefully removed the ring. When she was in her bear form, she slipped it into her muzzle and kept it under her tongue. This time, on his return, the prince was in despair. How would he ever find his lady love? Fear of swallowing the ring subdued the bear's laughter, but she still got a good kicking for the sounds of chuckling that emerged from beneath the table.

In the days before tea had reached these islands, a hot cup of chicken soup was the answer to a crisis. The prince ordered it and the bear shuffled off to prepare it. Fortunately, no other servant saw her spitting into the cup. When the prince had drunk the soup, he discovered the ring. How could it have got there? As she had served it, he asked the bear.

'My Prince, the ring travelled by starlight drawn by the four dapple grey steeds that outpaced a mighty wind.'

Then he looked into the bear's eyes and recognised his dancing partner. This time he did not kick the bear, he kissed her. The bear skin fell away and there before him was the woman he loved. Before long there was another ball and that was at their wedding. The guest of honour was the bear princess's father. When their first child was born, the princess's old nurse was invited to be the baby's godmother, and she also came to work for them in the nursery. They all lived happily ever after.

Field and Farm

As Drunk as a Pig

Free-range pigs rootling in apple orchards is a sight redolent of the rural idyll. The pigs are especially happy in this setting when the warm autumn sunshine has rotted the windfalls enough to turn them alcoholic. At that time of year, sheep, cattle and pigs can be quite entertaining under the influence of those fruits that weren't officially turned into cider.

There was one pig owner, however, who followed the example of his extraordinary pig all year round, which was easy for him to do because he owned a pub. His pig was unusual in that it had six legs and people used to come from quite a distance to admire this marvel. The publican encouraged these visitors because, having made the journey, they inevitably increased his trade. However, no matter how many visitors the pig had, their revenue could not make up for the loss of stock that the publican's drinking took out of the business.

As he drank more, he became more incapable, and his wife decided to step in to save the pub before he drank it into the ground. It was she who ran everything, from ordering supplies to serving customers. No matter how crafty she was in her attempts to limit his consumption, she was no match for the cunning of a dedicated alcoholic. On one occasion he was so drunk that he thought he had better go and sleep it off. He also feared his wife's scolding and threats, and knew he needed to hide somewhere. It was surprising that he managed to have these rational thoughts at all, given the state he was in.

The proud owner of the six-legged pig staggered to the sty, and let the animal out into the orchard that lay behind the pub. He then took up residence where the animal had been, covered himself with some wisps of straw and fell into the longed-for sleep. His snores were such that they in no way alerted his wife to the fact that it was no pig that awaited the little band of visitors and their hostess.

They stared speechless at the drunken landlord, who made up for their silence by his most hog-like sounds. His wife wished that the ground would swallow her up when one of the group exclaimed, 'I've never seen a pig as drunk as that in all my life, and that so early in September!'

Someone else tried to smooth things over: 'There, there missus, we won't be telling anyone how disappointed we are that the beast has two legs too few instead of two legs too many.'

'And they no use to anyone!' said another.

How Pigs Saved a Prince

Deep in the forest sat a man, his head in his hands. Around him a herd of pigs snuffled and rootled contentedly in the dappled shade. The man was in despair. If anyone had seen him in clothes so ragged that any beggar would despise them, they would not have been able to believe that this man was heir to the throne.

Not so long ago, he had returned from studies abroad and had contracted leprosy, for which there was then no cure. Lepers were banished from society, travelling together, warning everyone of their approach by ringing bells so that no one else would catch the disease they carried. They lived like beggars, hoping for alms. It was one of these bands that Prince Bladud was forced to join. However, when they asked him his story not only was he not believed, he was mocked. He could not bear to be shunned by all those he had known in his former life only to be mocked by fellow sufferers. He left the band of lepers and wandered on alone.

At last he came upon a remote farm where, by good chance, the farmer was in need of a swineherd for the summer. In those days pigs were herded to forage in the forest for most of the year. It was a lonely occupation that few wanted – but ideal for a leper – and the prince was grateful. At first all went as well as could be expected, but one dreadful day he discovered that in tending the pigs, they had caught his ailment. Their skins were covered with the pale blotches of leprosy. What could he tell the kind farmer who had entrusted them to him? That is why he was sitting in despair.

Eventually he decided to drive them further into the forest – perhaps the farmer, when he didn't return, would think that they had been attacked by wolves. He didn't know how long he would be able to survive when the cold weather came. It was the beginning of autumn, already the leaves were turning. He came to a part of the forest that somehow seemed to have retained the summer's warmth. Even the leaves were greener, but there was a strange smell in the air. The pigs snuffled up the scent and rushed towards a pit in the forest floor from which smoke seemed to be rising. To Prince Bladud's alarm the entire herd threw themselves into the pit.

When he had caught up with them, he discovered that it was not smoke, but steam. The pit was oozing and bubbling with hot, odorous mud and the pigs were wallowing in it. How they loved that strange place, hardly even emerging to forage. The prince was content to let them do as they pleased, because he too was able to keep warm in the steam-laden air in that distant glade that seemed to hold winter at bay. After a few days, the pigs stopped wallowing and the mud flaked away from their hides. The prince was looking idly at the pink skin showing through and then a realisation stirred – their skins shouldn't be pink! What had happened to those unsightly blotches of fungus-white leprosy? The warm mud with its strange sulphurous smell must have cured them. What harm if he tried it himself? Almost immediately, his skin started to improve. In a few days he too was cured.

He drove the herd back to the farmer and returned to court. Reinstated as heir to the throne, his first act was to reward the kindly farmer with a gift of land. Then he bought all the pigs so that they would not be slaughtered and were able to live out their natural lives in porcine luxury. Next he turned that muddy pit into springs where people could come for treatments and where cures could be made from the rich mud with its medicinal properties. So popular and effective were these waters that a town soon grew around them, which we now call Bath. It is the only place with hot springs in Britain and people still come to immerse themselves in these uniquely healing waters.

The Thieving Goat

Of all the sleepy little villages in Ireland only one relied on a goat as its singular source of excitement. Billy was considered a loveable rogue by his doting owner, but to everyone else there was no doubt as to why the Devil so resembled a goat. A Houdini amongst herbivores, Billy was uncontainable by any rope, pen, fence or device invented by farming kind. He would flaunt his latest escape by swimming across the pond rather than skirting it, as though to tell everyone that if they were thinking of building a moat to keep him in, they could think again.

Once free he would use his enhanced powers of mobility to get into the places that no other creature had reached. This was, of course, to find things to eat, although why Billy chose to eat most of what he stole was a mystery. It is true that the uncharitable would have said that undergarments from Mrs O'Brien's washing basket should have been on their way to the compost heap anyhow. However, his having gained entry to the church and eaten half the prayer books before he was discovered, proved beyond any reasonable doubt that he was the Devil incarnate.

The day came when Billy was no longer the focus of attention. A child of the village, now a man in his prime, had returned from America, where, like so many of his generation, he had gone to make his fortune. It certainly seemed that he had succeeded, as Liam O'Flaherty had gifts for everyone. At first people were awestruck, then grateful, and finally jealous. He never left the house before donning a new outfit, which made all the young girls swoon with admiration whilst at the same time being eaten up with envy. The young men ground their teeth as they knew they could never compete with this nouveau riche prodigal son. It was even more galling that his arrival coincided with the announcement that there would be a dance in a neighbouring village.

The young people prepared for this feverishly, the greater efforts being made by those with fewer resources. Girls shimmied down the riverbank to collect that particular shade of mud that, when it was smoothed on their legs, would resemble the nylon stockings they could never afford. Younger sisters would then draw a line on the backs of their legs with a stick dipped in moistened coal dust, to resemble seams. If these wavered from the straight and narrow, there was hell to pay, as the whole process would have to be repeated.

Young men, perhaps for the first time that year, would work the pump handle for each other and share a cracked mirror for their toilette. This consisted mainly of waxing their moustaches, but not by melting down their everyday tallow candles. If they were in a position later to snatch a kiss from some lucky maiden, they didn't want to taint the moment with the smell of rancid mutton fat. However, if some beeswax candles were found to be missing from the church, Billy could always be blamed.

In those frugal times, people had to make do with giving their patched and darned Sunday best a shake and a brush. Not so Liam. He triumphantly produced a flannel shirt of the brightest crimson and told his fawning mother to wash it. There it hung on the washing line, causing all the swains in the village to break the tenth commandment. How they longed to possess it. But they also knew that if they stole it, they could never get away with wearing it. As the day slipped into evening, Liam went to get the shirt off the line. It wasn't there, but Billy was. There the goat stood, calmly eyeing the shirt's previous owner with liquid topaz eyes. His jaws were working steadily and Liam was just in time to see a flash of crimson disappear.

The shouting and swearing brought people running, by which time Liam had seized his weapon. Billy had been threatened with a pitchfork before, and was not going to disturb himself enough to upset his digestion. However, when the other villagers arrived on the scene, Billy sensed a turn in the tide of his fortunes. With animal instinct, he realised that the multitude was eager, at last, to see his demise. The crowd was closing in, and it may have been that in their collective hostile gaze, Billy revisited all his previous crimes. With one leap he cleared the garden wall. Some scrambled after him, the more sedate used the gate, but the whole population was in pursuit.

Billy knew he couldn't be outdistanced, but he also knew that he was outnumbered. By now other weapons had appeared amongst his enemies, who were fanning out to head him off should he attempt to run for home. On he skittered – towards the railway line. Renowned for his surefootedness, the crowd gasped as Billy's hoof caught fast between the tracks. It was more a gasp of hope than horror. Sounds of glee then mingled with those of an approaching train. Billy was trapped. Billy was done for.

His owner flung himself face down to avoid seeing the inevitable – everyone else pressed forward. What luck that Billy was about to meet with the only train of the day! Now it could be seen as well as heard. The tracks started to sing and the goat started to shudder and shake. Then Billy vomited up the crimson shirt. Before it fell, he caught it between his teeth and vigorously swept it from side to side. The engine driver saw the red flag and threw on the brakes. With a grinding and screaming the train stopped just feet in front of Billy. Up the line it was expected that the train would have passed by then. The points changed and Billy was free. Which only went to show, as everyone observed, that the Devil takes care of his own.

The Cattle from the Lake

A young man lived by Llyn y Fan Fach lake in Wales. Its name means 'the Lake of the Small Hill' and you can see that a smaller hill seems to rise from the side of the water, the whole being almost surrounded by towering slopes. He would bring his flocks to this gentler slope to graze and drink from the lake.

One windless evening, he noticed ripples on the lake's surface. Then he saw a figure emerging from the water. A beautiful woman walked towards him. She smiled and held out her arms, before turning and disappearing back beneath the water. The young man told his mother what had happened, hardly knowing whether he had dreamed it all. The old woman listened and told him that he must bring some bread, baked by his own hand, if he wanted to entice the lake maiden onto solid ground. He had never made bread before; his mother had always done the baking. Nevertheless, with his mother's instructions, he managed to make some rough bread and took it to the lake shore the following evening.

Between waiting and hoping, he looked out anxiously over the water. There were the ripples again, the beautiful young woman walking towards him, coming closer to the shore this time. Her smile was a path of sunlight on the water. He waded through it until he was close enough to give her the bread. Her hands were like the water lilies that grew on the southern shore. Her teeth as she bit into the bread were like the little white pebbles amidst the shingle. The she spat it out.

'Too hard baked for me is your bread!' she said, but she was laughing as she turned from him and disappeared beneath the water.

The young man told his mother what had happened. She too laughed. Then she watched him try again at baking bread. He was careful not to leave it as long in the oven, eager to take it out as soon as the yeasty fragrance filled the room.

Next evening the lake maiden was there again, this time even closer to the shore. Knee-deep he handed her the bread, willing himself to be that crust touching her mouth. She spat it out.

'Too soft baked for me is your bread!' Her laughter swooped like a gull as she turned and disappeared.

His mother showed no surprise, and watched smiling as her son pulled a golden loaf from the oven. He took it to the lake at the appointed time – surely there was by now a tryst? This time she stood ankle-deep before him as he splashed to meet her. Her skin was smoother than any shell, gleaming like starlight on water. She took the bread, bit, swallowed. Then she looked at him deeply, deeper than any lake, as she bit and swallowed until the loaf was all gone: 'Good is your bread for me, no longer too hard or too soft. If you are willing, I will share your home and your hearth. I will share my life with your life on one condition, and if you break it I will return to my home beneath the waters of Llyn y Fan Fach. If you strike me three times I will be lost to you forever.'

The young man couldn't believe his good fortune when he heard these words. Again he wondered if he had been dreaming. But now the lake maiden was out of the water standing by him on dry land. Then he believed that surely he must be dreaming, as he saw her stretch her arms towards the water and begin to call. Her sing-song voice rose and fell like rising waves in the winds of autumn. He could not understand the words. Then he realised that she was chanting a stream of names. As she chanted, cattle emerged from the lake, each coming to the calling of its own name. There were great bulls, cows, heifers and calves. They were of every colour and marking he had ever seen and more. A great herd followed them home. None had ever seen the like of the cattle that had come from below the waters of the Lake of the Small Hill.

The couple were happy. Due to the dowry of cattle, the young husband was richer than he could have imagined. The cows' milk, always plentiful, was the wonder of the country. He could afford to buy his old mother anything she had ever wanted and everything she never knew she wanted. Time passed. Soon after their first son was born, they were guests at a wedding. The congregation rose as the bride entered the church, all except for the woman of the lake. Embarrassed at this sign of disrespect, her husband nudged her. She looked at him deeply as she had at their third meeting, but this time her look was darkened with sadness.

'I did not rise with respect for the bride because I know that before the year is out she will betray her husband with another man. You have now struck me once, so have a care.'

Her husband then realised that his wife had the second sight and did not question her further. He took care not to strike her again, and they raised their child happily along with his little brother who arrived soon after. A few years passed and they were guests at the christening of the couple whose wedding they had attended. As the priest blessed the baby, the woman of the lake wept loudly. Her shocked husband grabbed her and hustled her out of the church.

'I was weeping for the child because although she is being blessed at this moment, I know that nothing will save her from a life of pain and sickness and an early grave. She will die before her seventh year. And that was the second time you struck me, so have a care.'

It was clear that the child was sickly and didn't thrive like others of her age. During that time a third son was born to the woman of the lake, but just as had been predicted, the little girl died. Everyone attended the funeral and as the small coffin was being lowered into the ground, the woman of the lake began to laugh. Appalled, her husband clapped his hand over her mouth and led her away.

'I was laughing with happiness because I could see that poor child being welcomed at the gates of heaven and that her suffering was over for all eternity. Now you have struck me a third time and it is time for me to keep my promise.'

She turned and walked towards the lake. Somehow, no matter how quickly he ran, her husband could not catch up with her. There she was by the shore. Then he heard her chanting that sing-song list of names that he had heard so many years before. But this time it was much longer because it contained the names of all the calves, some now cows or bulls with offspring of their own, that had been born to the first of her dowry herd. A tide of cattle swept over the little hill towards the water. Even a newly flayed calfskin, stretched on a wall in an outhouse, regained its form, and the calf trotted off to join the herd. The man watched helplessly as all the cattle disappeared into the lake, followed by his wife, who did not once turn to look at him.

Their three sons grew into young men, helping their father on the now depleted farm. The brothers would often walk along the lake shore together. The eldest was now the same age as their father when he and the lake maiden first met. One evening, they saw their mother walking towards them. She began to teach them about the healing properties of all the plants to be found in the country. She gave them the knowledge of how to use every herb, shrub and plant for every ailment. Most of these were unknown at that time.

The three brothers later shared this knowledge with their father and their skill at healing every kind of illness soon became known throughout the land. They became known as the physicians of Myddfai, which is the name of the village close to where the local ruler created a centre for them to practice their art. Some say that they were so successful because their medical knowledge had been assisted by the second sight inherited from their mother. Certainly they founded a dynasty of famous healers in the tradition of the hereditary physicians that was the norm for that period. Some of their cures were written down in the fourteenth century. They can be found in the *The Red Book of Hergest*, which is held in Oxford's Bodleian library.

Faithful Gelert

Prince Llewelyn loved to hunt and found it hard to hide his pride when courtiers mentioned that he had the finest pack of hounds in all of Wales. One morning he was due to hunt, but none of the servants were available to look after his baby son. His wife was ill and being tended in another part of the castle so as not to pass on the sickness to the baby, who was left with only his young wet nurse. Llewelyn decided therefore to leave his favourite hound, Gelert, to guard the child.

On returning from the hunt the prince went first to check on the baby. He knew that something was wrong because he passed the wet nurse, who was weeping hysterically. He rushed into the room where he had left his child and found everything in disorder. Furniture had been overturned, including the crib, and blood had spattered the walls and pooled on the floor. But there was Gelert wagging his tail in greeting. Llewelyn looked around for his son but couldn't see him anywhere. It was then that he noticed the blood staining Gelert's muzzle and clotting his breast. The horror of what must have happened made him draw his sword quicker than he had ever done for any foe. With Gelert's trusting eyes still gazing into his and his tail still drumming on the bloodied floor, his master plunged the blade into the hound's breast. The howls as he died brought people running from all parts of the castle.

Beneath these anguished sounds, the man heard another – the cries of a baby. They were coming from beneath the crib. The father flung it away and found his son. Beside him was stretched a dead wolf, his throat torn out by a dog's teeth. It was only then that Llewelyn understood what had really happened – how his faithful hound had defended his son against all the odds, and how death had been his only reward, meted by the one he loved the most.

Servants and courtiers flooded into the room to find their prince holding the baby with tears streaming down his face. Some said it was in relief for his son's life being saved, but most said it was because of the terrible way he had betrayed his faithful friend. Llewelyn was so remorseful that he ordered a grave be made for Gelert outside the castle. Beside it there was a stone inscribed with the terrible story of how he had died. You can visit the place where all of this happened. It is Beddgelert, in Wales. The name means 'Gelert's Grave', which you can also see, although many visitors do not realise that they are looking at a recent recreation of it.

Cat against Rat

Dick Whittington was a newcomer to London. His brother had inherited, leaving him with nothing, so he made his way to the capital to make his fortune. In those days coming to that great city from rural Gloucestershire would have been like arriving in another country. He had been told, ever since he first learned to speak, that the streets of London were paved with gold. However, high up on Highgate Hill, with the spreading, smoking metropolis beneath him, he found that this was not so and turned his back on the city that had held such hope. It was evening and suddenly, all through that great city, the church bells rang out for Vespers. In their joyous chorus, Dick distinctly heard them ring out, 'Turn again, Dick Whittington, who three times Mayor of London will be, turn again, turn again.'

As he did so, the last rays of the setting sun emerged from a bank of cloud. When the pealing of the bells died away, not only the streets but the buildings too were lined with gold. At these good omens Dick stayed and looked for work, but so many were also looking that it was hard to find. At last he found a position in a house with a kindly master who paid little heed to what the servants got up to.

So it was that Dick was at the beck and call of a cruel and slovenly cook. Maybe it was because this lackadaisical cook was also too lazy to implement even the most basic hygiene of the time, that the household was even more overrun with rats than was usual, and that is saying quite a lot for those days. Harried all through the day, Dick barely slept at night for the rats that ran all over him as he tried to rest on his straw mattress.

As soon as he could, he acquired a cat. Tom was a ratter par excellence. He started in the attic where Dick slept, and having been the scourge of every pitter-pattering rodent in that part of the house, he spread his talents elsewhere. Dick's master and daughter were delighted – they had never lived in a rat-free abode, and even the cook was grudgingly pleased. Intrepid Tom became a regular sight around the district, riding on Dick's shoulder when he ran errands for his master. Alderman Fitzwarren made his fortune from the boats that discharged their exotic cargoes in London's great port. In those days every ship was overrun with rats, some species even bringing outbreaks of plague that swept through the country from the Middle Ages to the seventeenth century.

Often Fitzwarren, as a valued customer, would be invited on board to dine with the captain. On one such an occasion, the rat problem was so bad that it would have been easier to spear one of those vermin on the point of their knives than the food that was being stolen from their plates. This gave Dick's master an idea, and he asked to borrow Tom.

By now the young man was beginning to develop some business sense, and for a small fee, equal to that of the price of the food lost to the feasting rats, he would be prepared to hire out Tom's services! Moreover, as Tom was as loyal as the most faithful of dogs, he would go nowhere without his master, and Dick would have to go too. The Alderman smiled at this budding of commercial acumen and this bond between servant and master.

He sent a message to the captain saying that in future any rat problem would be dealt with before they dined. He soon returned to the afflicted vessel with Dick, who was accompanied by Tom riding in his usual style. Their host showed them into his cabin, which was heaving with rats, food already having been laid out to tempt them.

The captain was a well-travelled man who had seen many marvels, including that of a thunderbolt that had become trapped in the hold during a storm, causing havoc as it ricocheted between the planks. As Tom set to work, he had, however, never seen one so purposeful. He might have been wondering how rats had turned into bats, with so many of them flying and flipping through the air. Tom believed that if a job was worth doing, it was worth doing properly, so all of his victims were quite dead before they landed. Furthermore, as speed, precision and delicacy were Tom's forte, not so much as a single cat hair was found in the rescued food being enjoyed by the three men. Their happy crunching of pork crackling and crab claws was echoed by Tom in his corner. As was his habit, he chewed his prey methodically from the nose down, leaving only the tail as a trophy, of which there must, by then, have been many thousands.

Tom's fame spread, he received many dinner invitations, and Dick was beginning to save money. Who knows how many outbreaks of plague Tom may have averted with his labours? In time, Dick was able to leave service and become a merchant himself. You may be certain that when at last he could afford his own ship, it was rat-free. There was no food wastage or rat-gnawed leaks and his crew was healthy.

Dick's fortunes grew and his pockets and strongboxes were full of gold. He finally understood why the streets of London were said to be lined with it. As he prospered, he could afford to take the risk of sending his vessels – for now he had several – on longer voyages. It was a bigger risk, but reaped larger profits if the ship wasn't lost at sea.

One journey took him all the way to Morocco, where the king was eager to establish trading routes with Northern Europe. Dick was even invited to dine with the king – except that nobody was eating very much at all because the palace had the worst infestation of rats ever known. In hot countries their breeding cycle is accelerated and this plague of vermin was making the most of the climate. Tom didn't wait to be asked, and dispatched the multitude with his usual terpsichorean prowess. The King of Morocco was delighted and paid Dick to stay longer to give Tom a chance to exercise his talents amongst his subjects. Soon there wasn't a rat to be seen in the whole of Tangier – perhaps word of the massacres had got around and many of the vermin had fled the city.

When it was time for Dick to leave, he didn't buy any cargo to trade in London. This was because the king had given him so many costly gifts that there was no room in the hold for anything else. Dick had become a wealthy and respected man, and as the bells had told him all that long time ago, he was thrice elected Mayor of London. In fact, Dick became mayor four times. The bells were unable to predict that apart from being elected thrice, on one occasion he was appointed by the king, following the untimely death of his predecessor whilst still in office.

If you go to Highgate Hill today, Dick is remembered in the naming of The Whittington Hospital. Outside is a statue of Tom with railings around it. No doubt these are to discourage the unfortunate attentions of passing dogs, rather than to keep Tom confined. Even in petrified form he would be able to clear them with one bound. Next to it is a pub called The Cat in which, until recent times, Tom's actual mummified body was to be seen in a glass case. This didn't reappear after the pub was refurbished and I asked after it. The landlord told me that the case had been broken whilst being moved, and the mummy had been put in an outbuilding temporarily. With all the upheaval it had been forgotten. When it had been rediscovered, it had unfortunately been so gnawed by rats that it was no longer possible to display it. This was all related without a trace of irony

The Donkey in a Basket

An old gypsy owned a donkey who was as much family pet as working companion. He would travel over the county with goods for sale packed into the donkey's panniers. A familiar and welcome sight, his customers would joke with him as to which was the older and greyer. If he had managed to sell his goods, he would sometimes give the smallest of the farm children a ride in the donkey's panniers.

When he wasn't travelling, the gypsy would make baskets out of willow of all shapes and sizes that his wife would nest together and sling over her back, selling them from door to door. It was then that the old donkey would get a rest. Then his master would mutter, part joking, part grumbling, his gnarled fingers busy with the withy wands, that he was the only one amongst them who never got any rest at all. The old man's fingers weren't as nimble as they used to be in their plaiting and weaving, and this was making him bad-tempered. Despite being pushed away several times, the donkey nevertheless persisted in his favourite game of trying to sneak up on him and chew his straw hat. When he accidentally tipped it over his master's eyes during a particularly tricky moment, the man lost his temper. Seizing a withy wand, he lashed out fiercely.

To his horror, the strength of the blow completely split the donkey in half, each half falling different ways like a sliced apple.

It was as well that his wife returned at that moment. She propped up the two halves so that they were close enough to lean into each other. Then she grabbed the slimmest and most supple of the withy wands and bound the two halves of the donkey round about with the flexible switches of willow, until he looked like he was wearing a basket. Just as willow will graft together, so did the donkey. Great was their relief when his halves grew together again.

An unexpected bonus was that the basket around his middle continued to sprout withies. This resulted in him always carrying a crop of these around with him, which made the gypsy's work much easier as this was a handier arrangement than having to forage for them.

Another Christmas Donkey

At the end of the summer the funfair moved on, taking its larger-than-life sights and sounds with it. The trampled field where it had been was left to its drab colours, bleached from the summer and browning with the coming of autumn. The tufts of grass that had survived the weight of the rides and the scuffing of many feet, swayed with the sighing wind already cold with the promise of winter. This year the field hadn't been left empty. The funfair had left something behind, a donkey that had worked for many years giving children rides.

The children looked forward to the fair every year, saved their pennies, vied with each other over how many rides they could go on. The raucous noise and gaudy colours were a joyful change in their humdrum lives. The donkey rides were always popular. The children who rode them were too young to see that the fair was all about making money, and their fun was at the expense of the overworked and underfed animals that carried them. This donkey had become lame through neglect and his owner hadn't thought him worth the expense of having his injury treated, so had abandoned him.

There wasn't much to eat in the field and as the weather grew colder even less grew. Fortunately, there was a ditch at its edge or he would have died of thirst. His lame leg was painful and he had to walk further to find food as the weather grew bleaker. Even worse than the pain and the hunger was the loneliness. Donkey had never been alone before. He loved the children who rode him, but now there was nobody. The empty days stretched into weeks and months. It was the time of year when the grey daylight glimmered fitfully into long cold nights.

Then there came a night when a brightness appeared in the sky. It came with a jingling sound that reminded Donkey of the acrobats and the dancing girls in the fair. Then he could smell other animals. Best of all he heard a human voice. Sometimes it was calling to the animals and sometimes laughing for the joy of it. Donkey could tell that the voice was kind. Santa Claus and his sleigh made a bumpy landing. Donkey was not afraid when the burly man hurried up to him. He nuzzled his sleeve and did not want to stop. Now he was shivering with pleasure instead of cold.

'We were flying over when I saw you. I was hoping that you could help me out. We only have a few more houses to do, so we can reach them on foot, but one of my reindeer is lame. I was hoping that you wouldn't mind doing a swap?'

Not only would Donkey have company, he could be useful again! Already he was moving towards the sleigh, trying hard to disguise his limp. Santa Claus soon had him harnessed up next to one of the reindeer, and they were off at a trot. How his injury pained him, but how proud he was to be helping Santa on Christmas Eve. Donkey couldn't keep up the pace and the sleigh had to go slower as it neared the end of its round. Santa Claus had noticed the donkey's condition and a worried frown puckered his usually jolly face. They had reached the last house. It was almost dawn.

'I'm going to leave you here, old fellow, no need to go back to that miserable field, thanks for all your help.'

Santa Claus remembered the house from last year. A family with a gaggle of children had recently moved in. The parents were vets. He removed the sack that had held presents from Donkey's back, but it wasn't quite empty. At the end of it there remained a wide scarlet satin ribbon. Santa Claus pulled it out and searched in his tunic for something to write with. Then he tied the ribbon round the donkey's neck. How proud Donkey felt. Nobody had ever given him a present before.

'You wait here, old fellow, it won't be long now. And thank you again, I'll know where to find you if I need you next time.'

There were those happy sounds of jingling and laughing again as the sleigh set off to collect the last of the reindeers. But there was also another voice. A child crying out, 'I saw him! I saw him!'

Then the sounds of hurrying steps, running, tripping, and squealing excited voices as the children burst out of the house.

Astonished silence greeted the donkey. The eldest reached for the ribbon. In the early light of Christmas morning she read,
    'With love from Father Christmas.'

Jack in a Sack

Three brothers lived on a farm. The two older ones were both greedy and lazy. The youngest was a happy-go-lucky chap who didn't seem to notice the cruel pranks his brothers played on him, or if he did, he didn't seem to mind. The older men plotted to get rid of him, because that way they would only have to share the proceeds of the farm with each other instead of splitting it three ways.

They came up with a plan, which was to tell him that they had found a way to get to Heaven. When they were there, they would be able to help themselves from the heavenly flocks of sheep and drive as many as they wanted back home. They held a sack open, so that it looked like a mouth of a tunnel, and told him that if he got into it, the quickest way to Heaven was to be thrown into the lake. On that calm summer's day, with not a single cloud in the sky, the lake resembled the sky itself and was certainly much easier to get to. Jack was very happy to be given this chance, especially when he was told that he could go first – which meant that he didn't have to carry his brothers to the lake in a sack. They would do that for him. Jack was heavier than they had anticipated and the older brothers developed a powerful thirst, so they decided to quench it halfway at a hostelry called The Woolsack. They explained to Jack that they would run on ahead and make sure that there were no rocks in the lake to impede their progress to Heaven, and that they would be back for him soon.

So Jack in his sack was left in a ditch by the roadside. To while away the time, he started to sing, and the lusty strains of 'The Lord is my Shepherd' were heard by another passer-by. Driving a flock before him, the sheep rustler was astonished to hear praises emanating from a sack, rather than cries for help. Curiosity overcame the need to get the stolen sheep out of sight, and he stopped to ask the sack's occupant what was going on. Jack told him everything that he had heard from his brothers. The sheep rustler's eyes gleamed with greed as he realised that he might be the better off for a far larger flock. He decided to try to bargain.

'My good friend, I can only pass this way the once, whereas you, being from these parts, can come back tomorrow. If you let me have your place in the sack, I will give you all my sheep that I have here, and you can increase them at your leisure.'

This sounded too good an offer to refuse, so Jack agreed. The sheep rustler untied the sack. After they had changed places, Jack tied it up again, and went home with the sheep.

Having refreshed themselves, the brothers returned to the ditch. The sheep rustler thought it prudent not to reply to any questions, lest a different voice be remarked upon. The brothers assumed he was asleep and grumbled about his weight all the way to the lake. There he was thrown into the deepest part that could be reached from the shore. The brothers returned home, well satisfied with their evil deed.

Great was their astonishment when they saw Jack and the sheep. How had he reached home before them with a flock to drive? How had he managed to remain completely dry? He explained to them that he could have had many more, but didn't think that he could drive them all by himself. Indeed, he had great trouble in preventing the rest of the Heavenly Flock from following their brethren, but promised his brothers that he would take them to the exact place where the others waited. Jack then cast a weather eye to the sky and suggested that it was too late to make that journey – better to set out in the morning.

Having safely penned the sheep, Jack fetched a sack in which he helped to carry his brothers, and they took it in turns to carry or be carried, for appearances sake, so as not to arouse his suspicions. A gentle breeze was blowing to keep them cool, which was just as well, as there were no stops at The Woolsack for refreshments – so eager were the older brothers to acquire their heavenly dues. They hurried along as best they could, each alternately cursing the weight of the other, their gaze fixed on the blue lake ahead. Jack, however, looked up from time to time and noted with satisfaction the fluffy white clouds that the breeze had brought and which he had anticipated the previous evening.

Eventually they reached the appointed place, a smooth rock jutting out over the water. However, neither of the greedy brothers would trust the other as to which should go first, so one was released from the sack until the matter was decided.

At that spot, the great rock sheltered the lake from the wind so that there was hardly a ripple on its surface. The reflection of those fluffy white clouds looked like so many lambs gambolling about just beneath the water. Knowing that they would never agree, and that if they did the other was not to be trusted anyway, the brothers took a running jump and splashed into the lake at the same time.

Jack rolled up the sack for other uses and made his way home. Pausing only for a short time at The Woolsack to refresh himself after his exertions, he returned to where the sheep greeted him with the affection due to a kinder master. All knew when they were better off, and if in due course Jack shared the proceeds of the farm with anyone else, it was with one of his own choosing.

But One Horse Missing

The farmer could never work out how his mare had foaled such a beauty. Of common stock herself, her colt was of a quality that had never been seen in those parts – not even at the horse fairs that were attended by dealers from afar. Always large and strong for his age, he would move with such a nimbleness and grace, his grey coat slipping like moonlight amongst the dappling orchard shadows. His owner couldn't account for it. He wondered if his dam had been covered unbeknownst by a different stallion – perhaps a passing gypsy's, they had fine horses after all. But that was unlikely, they were so proud and careful of them.

When the time came, he took to saddle and bridle as though he had been waiting for them. He won every class in every show he entered. He came first in every race and was the envy of all who admired horseflesh. Strange to say, the farmer never gave him a name.

'There'll be time enough for that, no hurry at all,' he would say when questioned about this omission.

The truth was that whenever he tried to think of a name, he could never quite hold onto a particular one in his mind. It was as though a whole herd of names came galloping towards him and as he tried to seize a particular one, it would slip past him like moonlight on the trunks of the apple orchard. This made entering competitions rather tricky, so the judges good humouredly registered the colt as 'Nameless'. So Nameless he became, and that was what he was known by.

Years passed and the farmer fell upon hard times. He risked losing the farm and needed money to pay off his debts. The horse, now in his prime, would fetch a good price. Of course, he didn't want to part with him, but he felt he had no choice. He prepared to leave for the horse fair that would be taking place on the far side of the great hill the next day. It was a long way as the hill was too steep to have any paths across it, and travellers had to make their way around its base. They left very early in the morning. The moon had set, but there were still plenty of stars in the sky. The farmer led the horse rather than riding. He wanted the animal to appear as fresh as possible for any buyers.

After much walking, the path narrowed as it squeezed itself past a great stone set into the hillside. It was there that another blocked their way. In the dawn light, the farmer could see that this was an old man.

'A fine horse and what is his name?' asked the stranger.

'My horse is Nameless.' His owner was not pleased by having his way blocked by this curious nobody.

'Nameless is it?' The farmer was further displeased at the knowing smile on the stranger's lips. 'Yes, Nameless you may be my friend, but Nameless you shall not be for long.'

Then a strange thing happened. The horse stretched out his neck and whickered softly the way horses greet one of their own. He blew into the stranger's ear and nuzzled his neck. His owner became even more disgruntled at this affection, shown to someone who behaved with more familiarity than he was entitled to. As though sensing his mood, the old man said, 'I mean no harm to man or beast. I'll give you a good price for your horse, paid in gold.'

He reached beneath his cloak and the gold dazzled in the early morning light. Maybe because he felt something uncanny about this stranger, or maybe because he felt wrong-footed, the farmer refused.

'Come, come, man, I know you are bound for the fair to sell him and I am offering you a good price. No one will offer you better. Why not save yourself a long journey and haggling over a worse bargain?'

But the farmer, by now as stubborn as stone, would not agree. As he led Nameless away, he heard the old devil cry out, 'I warn you, you'll not get a better price!'

Not only was he not offered a better price, he wasn't offered any. Many came to admire the animal, even to run their hands over him and look into that huge mouth. But when it came to naming a price it was as though their thoughts stampeded away from them and they heard their enfeebled voices mutter, 'Well good luck and good day to you' as they melted into the crowd.

The horse fair was over and he hadn't made a sale. Wearily he made his way back home. Now it was the sunset that was lighting the great stone by the path. There stood the old man, waiting for them. Nameless whinnied a greeting.

'Would you think better of it and sell him to me now?'

The farmer was glad to and took the old man's gold. Then as he tried to hand over the reins the new owner said, 'I'll need your help for a short while yet.'

He took a twisted staff from beneath his cloak and struck the great rock. There was a groaning and a grinding as it split into two. The whole hill seemed to shudder as it opened to reveal a tunnel that was lit up by the low evening light. A duller gleam within echoed the sunset. The farmer could see that it was from a huge metal object, its rounded shape bulging over the narrow passage. The old man took a length of cloth and tied it around the horse's mouth, binding his jaws together.

'Help me to guide the horse past the bell. We must make sure that not a single hair on his hide touches it and you must be as careful with your own person. But we must also make haste, I do not want to leave the gates open for any longer than can be helped.'

The farmer led Nameless and the old man brought up the rear. As they entered the tunnel, they blocked out what little light remained. The old man raised his staff and a blue light glowed all about them. Slowly, carefully, they passed the bell and followed the tunnel as it led down, under the hill, into a huge cavern.

The light blossomed to fill that space and the farmer marvelled to see that in the middle lay a circle of sleeping men. Warriors of old they seemed to be, each with a hand on the pommel of a sword. In their midst was another, even larger than those mighty twelve. He too wore a sword belt, but the scabbard was empty. Instead his hand rested on a horn slung about his neck. Years beyond counting had these sleepers lain there. Through the ages their hair and beards had grown like silver rivers, flowed down their bodies and swirled around their feet. As their guardian moved closer, the light from his staff picked out the gossamer cobwebs that covered them like a shroud, despite the gentle rise and fall of their breath. Tenderly, he leaned forward over the circle and pulled a veil of cobwebs away from the greatest warrior's face, lifting it to reveal a glimmering circlet on his brow. Then he bent, and gentle as a mother with a newborn, he placed a kiss there.

The farmer looked beyond that group, and at the limit of his vision he could make out that the round walls of the cavern were divided into stalls. Twelve of these each held a horse, all of them greys, their proud necks drooped in sleep. The thirteenth stall was empty. Now he realised why Nameless' mouth had been bound – it was to prevent him also whinnying a greeting to his sleeping brethren. Without needing to be told, he led him to the empty stall. Already his gait was faltering and his huge eyes half closed with the spell of sleep that was overcoming him. The man's heart lifted to know that although he was to be parted from his friend, Nameless would live on long after his own end.

The blue light came closer and lit up a small tunnel he had not noticed. The old man gestured towards it and whispered that he should fill his pockets with as much as he could carry as long as he could do so silently. There treasure gleamed, countless precious objects and heaps of gold coin. The farmer did not hesitate as the staff was held high so that he could see what he was doing. With a nimbleness that he thought his work-thickened fingers had long forgotten, he packed his coat so skilfully that not a chink or tinkle was heard.

Unhampered by the weight of the treasure, he quickly made his way back to the first tunnel with the blue light following so that he could see his way. Eager to escape with this fortune, he forgot to be careful when passing the bell. His coat brushed against it and the great bell, silent for ages, stirred in its sleep. Its voice shimmered into the dimming blue cavern. In that sound the farmer heard the cries and whispers of countless people, the roaring of the oceans and the sighing of the wind in the trees. He heard the rushing of rivers, the hiss of rain, he heard the song of every bird of field and forest. As those echoes faded, a huge voice rang out, 'Is it time, my friend? Has the time come at last?

At that mighty sound it was as though his limbs had lost all their power and his mind the will to move them. No longer able to breathe, he could feel his heart slowing, the grip on his bundle weakening as his fingers became numb with an icy cold. And then came the answer: 'No my liege, it is not time, the time has not yet come!'

Then the farmer could move. He ran, shooting out from under the hill, past the rock at its entrance, into the night. The grinding of the rock's closing shook every bone in his body and made his jaws judder. He was free and he was rich and the farm was saved.

Of course, everyone wanted to know how he had come by his sudden fortune, and he was happy to tell them over a few drinks, which, now that he was the wealthiest in the parish, he paid for. Whilst he was buying, they were happy to hear that story again and again. In time the money ran out and he wondered how he could have let such good fortune run through his fingers.

'Or down his throat,' as the few teetotallers amongst the villagers said.

Sometimes he would return to that narrow curving path to where the great rock stood, sentinel to the cavern where king and warriors slept under the hill. Although he banged his fists on the stone and called 'Nameless' until his voice was cracked, nothing and nobody ever answered him.

If you go to that village today, the one that lies under the great hill, you will easily find its only pub. There sits an old farmer who looks up eagerly whenever anybody enters, in case it is a stranger. Then, if it is his lucky day, that stranger will offer to buy him a drink in exchange for being told the story of the King Under the Hill.

Whale Music

We often refer to the sounds of the sea in musical terms. It is thought that an inspiration for the slow airs in Irish music, so evocatively sung or played on bagpipes, came from the Blasket Islands off the Kerry coast. The fishing boats were made of wooden ribs covered with animal skin, usually cow, or amongst poorer people, sealskins. These acted as a membrane through which the rowers would hear the songs of the migrating Humpback and Minke whales, whose haunting melodies would be echoed in their folk music. Another nautical music-making story comes from the neighbouring coast of Wales.

A fisherman was caught in a storm and thought that he would never see land again. He was washed overboard and buffeted about in the dark watery world that had no direction and no stillness. Preparing for death, he silently spoke his last prayer.

He must have passed over into the world that lies beyond this one, because he found that he could hear. He was listening to sounds the like of which he had never heard before. They were otherworldly, sometimes eerie and sometimes so sweet they could only be angelic. He felt heavenly warmth on his face after cold depths, stillness after endless turmoil. It was good to lie there, comforted, listening.

At last, the sun becoming rather too warm, he opened his eyes and saw a pebbly beach. Heaven must also have a coast as well as a garden. It was good to see something he could recognise, but when he tried to move, to his dismay, it seemed that he was trapped in a cage. Had he become a prisoner?

What took him some time to realise was that the sea had carried him, still alive but unconscious, onto an island beach. A wave had flung him with such force that he had washed up inside the ribcage of a whale carcass. The mighty animal had died long ago but his skeleton had survived, picked clean by birds and scoured by the weather. Those exquisite sounds were being made by the wind playing amongst the whale's bones. The different notes ran up and down, high and low, according to the gradually increasing and decreasing lengths of the ribs.

There was enough to survive with on that rocky shore whilst the fisherman waited and hoped for rescue. His only company was the voice of the wind playing to him through the whale's ribs. When there was no wind he was lonely, so he found a way of making cords from clothes, from seaweed and creeping cliff vines. He attached these to the bones and was able to make sounds by pulling them. Somehow, through the movement of his fingers, there was another voice speaking to him. Sometimes when the wind blew, he too spoke to the wind in this way, and they would play a duet together.

When at last he was rescued, he didn't forget about the music he had discovered. He found other bones, made other cords all of a more manageable size. People loved the music he played on them, so he started to make these instruments small enough to travel about his homeland with. In time people made others with wood and even strings of metal. This is the story of how the first Welsh harp was created.

How the Narwhal Became

Until well into the nineteenth century in Europe, it was believed that the magnificent single curly horn of the narwhal whale came from unicorns. Even today they are called 'The Unicorn of the Sea'. Although they do not migrate from the Arctic Circle, traders, trappers and tides would bring their almost priceless horns south. These were amongst the most prized possessions of European monarchs as it was believed that they had magical powers, and if placed in drink or food, could detect poison. Legend has it that Queen Elizabeth I owned one of these 'unicorn horns'. This object would also have been strongly associated with her complimentary sobriquet 'The Virgin Queen' as it was believed that only a virgin could entrap a unicorn, which in her presence would be compelled to lay its head in her lap.

It is a happy and rare moment for a storyteller when fact imitates fiction. This happened at The Shipwreck Museum on the Isle of Wight when the author came across an exhibit that could have come straight from the following story. Sadly, it did not comprise the original Ark, but a more recent vessel named The Pique. *There you can see the narwhal's horn that was found embedded in the ship after an Atlantic voyage. Her logbook described her being attacked by a sea monster, which we now know to have been a narwhal. Curiously, if the French word* Pique *is spelled in a certain way it means 'stung', it also means 'spade' as in the card suit.*

> *The animals went in two by two*
> *Hurrah! Hurrah!*
> *The animals went in two by two*
> *Hurrah! Hurrah!*
> *The animals went in two by two*
> *Never too many and never too few*
> *And they all came into the Ark*
> *For to get out of the rain ...*

Long before any monarchs lived in Europe, Old Noah had been given his orders. These included, with the exception of a few sheep, to allow all animals on board the Ark, one of each gender, as long as their usual home was not a watery one.

Just as this story did not get into the Old Testament, neither did the unicorn get onto the Ark. Although swimming alongside, begging to be taken on board, passage was refused on the grounds that Unicorn was only to be found in the singular. As Unicorn was not in a position to rectify this uniqueness, a deep sense of injustice was felt. Unicorn accordingly rammed the Ark's hull with that remarkable horn, and the vessel sprang a leak.

The leak was discovered by Mrs Noah, who realised that action needed to be taken quickly. She grabbed a passing dog, being about the right size and trainable, and shoved its nose into the hole to serve as a bung.

'Stay!' she ordered, and this command became the first recorded instance of dog training.

The dog obliged, but the hole grew bigger. She pulled the dog away, rolled up her sleeve and stuck her elbow in the leak instead. However, this meant that she couldn't move away to find a more permanent solution, and she could also feel that the hole was getting bigger. She called for help and at last Noah heard her.

He hurried off to get his toolkit, but as he never put anything away after finishing a job, he ended up running hither and thither looking for what he needed. He kept forgetting where he had put down what he had just found whilst in pursuit of the next item. Rushing around without nails whilst holding a hammer, he managed to be without either when holding a spare piece of board. Meanwhile, the leak was getting larger. On his next hurry past, Mrs Noah grabbed him in desperation. She pulled down his trousers and any happy anticipation he may have had was short-lived as she pushed him against the side – and squashed his bottom into the leaking hole. There it provided an adequate bung for the duration of the voyage. Ample meals were provided in situ, lest any loss of weight made it less efficacious.

That is why, from that day to this day, a dog's nose is always cold and so is a woman's elbow. That is also why a man will stride into a room, swirl his coat tails aside or hitch up his jacket, and angle his bottom as close to the fire as he can.

As for Unicorn, that unhappy creature kept swimming and swimming until its legs were quite worn away with the effort and the pressure of the water. Although legend does not tell us, it could be that Unicorn was female, so that when her legs were quite worn away Narwhal was left swimming in the ocean, parthenogenesis ensuring the multiplying of her kind.

That is also why, from that time to this time, we can search the wild wide world and never a unicorn will we find.

Saved by a Seal

Anthropologists and scholars of traditional narrative agree that the commonest stories to be found along the coasts of Britain, Ireland and Scandinavia are those of selkies or seal people. In Gaelic and Gallic the words for 'seal' can be roughly translated as 'hound of the sea' or 'sea dog'. This descriptive name tallies with their dog-like characteristics such as their curiosity about and affinity for humans. It also acknowledges, long before any evolutionary scientists, a common ancestor with those of their canine cousins.

Their similarities to humans include the sound of their voices, a love of music and being the only animal that can shed tears.

Amongst even the poorest communities along the seaboard, living in the harshest conditions where death from hunger or exposure was a real threat, there was often a taboo against killing seals. Despite their blubber providing food, light and heat, and their coats being used for clothing and skins for boats, to kill a seal was considered unlucky or unwise. There are countless tales of fisherman and children being rescued by seals, just as there are of people rearing lost seal pups. The author declares her bias, having swum with a particularly friendly and playful seal who spent his leisure hours courting tourists and on other occasions being followed along the shore by those seals to whom she was singing.

Given that there are entire volumes devoted to the vast collection of seal and selkie stories, it is a challenge to know which stories to include in this small book, whose remit is to tell stories of zoological rather than magical animals. However, the folklore and narratives of this extraordinary animal are inextricably woven with the selkies, who are seals in the sea and humans on land. For millennia, right up until living memory, these shape- and element-shifting creatures were perceived to be as natural as gulls or herring. The following stories are an attempt to straddle the twin paths created by Nature and people's response to the natural world – twin paths so seldom parallel, so often intertwined.

A fisherman was alone in his boat. Although he was not far from the shore, a great storm suddenly blew up from behind the headland and the wind blew him out to sea. The huge waves soon overwhelmed his craft and he was thrown into the water. He could hardly tell whether it was day or night, so dark was the sky. Neither did he know which way the shore lay so even if he were able to keep afloat, he didn't know which direction to make for. What he did know was that he didn't have long to live.

Just as he was beginning to swallow water, he felt something solid under him. At first he thought it was his boat, but as the great solid shape lifted him out of the water, there was another head just in front of his own. Beneath him was a bull seal. Hour after hour he was kept afloat by that powerful animal, who never seemed to tire. At last the storm passed and then the seal started to swim purposefully. There was the overturned boat. The seal dived, leaving the man half floating, half drowning for a few moments. He dived beneath the boat, surging up with his huge strength to right it. Then he dragged the fisherman by his clothes until he was alongside. Gently and firmly, the huge beast rolled up against him and heaved him into the craft before disappearing.

It was some time before the man could piece together how long he had spent adrift, day after day, not knowing whether his thirst was a worse torment than the cold. Back in his village he had been given up for lost and a wake had already been held for him.

Over the sea, in another country, a lighthouse keeper, ever vigilant, had been disturbed by what sounded like a foghorn. He couldn't understand it because there was no fog. Looking for the source of the sound, he saw a huge seal roaring on the rocks. Moreover, it kept rushing towards the lighthouse and away again towards the water, just like a dog urgently summoning its master to show him something. Realising that some action was required, the keeper seized his binoculars and could just about make out a small craft in the distance. He grabbed some necessities and set off towards it in his own boat, the seal plunging ahead of him. As the man could not row nearly as fast as the animal could swim, the seal kept returning as though to chivvy him along.

At last he drew alongside the fisherman's boat, and was just in time to save him. After he was able to drink some water, he sipped brandy while wrapped in a blanket. The seal had disappeared. It took the fisherman some weeks to regain his strength after his ordeal. The lighthouse keeper nursed him back to health and was glad of the company as his was a lonely life. As his health improved, his guest helped with the chores and eventually was able to work his passage back to his own island. Three months after his disappearance he turned up in his home village. How everyone rejoiced to see him and marvelled at his story. No one on that island ever killed a seal again.

The Origin of the Selkies

Long, long ago, before people had learned to put to sea in boats, the sea belonged only to its creatures. Beneath the waves lived the king and queen of the sea, who had many children. They all had huge shining dark eyes, and to look into any of them was like seeing the glimmering treasure that lay within the sea caves at the bottom of the ocean. They loved to play in the rolling surf and listen to the music of the sea. Their sweet singing was such that they could calm any storm or rouse the waves to crashing splendour.

The queen died and although her heartbroken husband knew that he would never be able to love anyone else, he decided to marry again for the sake of his motherless children. He chose a sea witch who lived in a deep cave beneath the seabed. She was glad to accept, as the position of queen would enable her to use her magical powers in any way she wished.

Soon she had concocted a spell with which to turn the king's children into the animal they most resembled with their playfulness and love of music. So it was that the children of the sea became seals. As with many spells, there is often a chink in the magic. Once a year, between dawn and sunset, the seals would come ashore, remove their sealskin coats and regain their human form. They would sing and play together on the rocks and beaches, and it would be only a matter of time before these selkies would be seen by a human.

Such was their beauty and so enchanting was their singing that any mortal who saw them would fall in love with one. This happened to a fisherman whose name is remembered yet, Roderic MacCodrum. Attracted by their singing that he had heard from afar, he came upon a group of selkies. He watched for a while but it didn't take him long to be smitten by one of their number. How he longed to join in and dance with her! But when he arose from behind the rocks, the selkies took fright. They ran for their sealskins and, seizing them, ran down to the water's edge. As soon as they threw them around their human bodies they became seals and took to the waves.

However, MacCodrum reached the pile of skins just as there was only one remaining – that of his beloved. He managed to seize it first, and without it she was compelled to remain on land with him. Having no other choice, she married him and they had many children.

That is how the selkies first became entwined with the human race. This happened wherever selkies came to land and many clans and tribes acknowledge their descent from selkie ancestors. Apart from various physical characteristics, signs of selkie blood include being irresistibly attractive and musically gifted. Just as any man may fall in love with a selkie woman seen on the strand, so do male selkies have a fascination for human women. They will appear on land, hard to distinguish from ordinary mortals unless you know what to look for, and will seduce the woman they fancy. They have even been known to sing a woman into an enchanted sleep, so that the first she knows about her seduction is when she finds herself pregnant.

> *'I am a man upon the land*
> *And I am a Selkie in the sea*
> *But when I'm far and far frae land*
> *My home it is in Sule Skerry.'*
> *'It was not well,' quoth the maiden fair –*
> *'It was not well indeed,' quoth he,*
> *' – That the great grey Selkie of Sule Skerry*
> *Should have come and got a bairn with me …'*

The Selkie Suitor

A father and daughter lived with no one else near in their cottage by the sea. They loved and cared for each other and worked hard. The old man often turned in before the young woman, never failing to bar the door before he did so. She would sit up with the flickering firelight for company.

One day she had been gathering seaweed on the beach and singing to the seals as she often did. She thought nothing of it when a great bull seal followed her along the shoreline. That night when her father had gone early to bed as was his habit, she thought she could hear music. Rising and falling like waves, the singing was carried on the wind. Wild it was, and desolate. She did not know if her heart was filled more with longing or loneliness. Then the barred door suddenly sprang open and a stranger stood at the threshold. Hospitality was law in that remote place, so, although she was frightened, she invited him in.

'You are welcome, Sir. Please forgive me for not waking my father, he is old and has been hard at work with poor fishing, his nets being so torn by the seals.'

'Are his nets made from horsehair?' came the surprising response.

'No Sir, they are not.'

'Are any ropes on his boat made of horsehair?'

'No, Sir, they are not. But please be welcome and take my father's seat by the fire. I heard the wind rising just now.'

'Thank you, but I will not sit by the fire, it is too warm for me.'

So she set her father's chair in a further corner. When she took his long grey coat from him, she could barely lift it to the hook. She had never touched anything so soft and heavy. For a moment she felt her eyelids grow heavy with sleep and a warm blush crept along her skin beneath her clothes.

'How warm your coat must be, Sir.'

'It serves me well, maiden, in all weathers.'

Then from his dark corner, he spoke to her for the rest of that night. She could barely tell if she was listening or dreaming, as her strange guest spoke as gently to her as the whispering foam on the sand. Just before dawn he took his coat and left.

When her father awoke she told him of all that had passed – all, that is, that she could remember. The beginning of the visit was somehow easier. He asked her to repeat the visitor's questions about horsehair ropes and nets, looking grave. The old man knew that only rope made of horsehair was strong enough to catch a seal. Then he felt the seat of his chair. His hand came away wet. He took a cloth and dried it, but it remained as wet as before. It was only when he mixed sand with a handful of salt and sprinkled them that the seat would dry. At that his face became graver still.

'I'll sit up with you tonight for when your visitor returns. It is not seemly that you receive male company alone.'

'What makes you think he will return tonight, Father?' she asked, as wistful as she was alarmed.

'Oh, he'll be back again, as sure as tides turn.'

Not long after he had barred the door, it sprang open and there was the man, his long coat swinging in the breeze from the open door. He stood at the threshold until invited in. As was polite, he spoke more to the eldest of the company.

'You have come from afar,' said the old man. 'Perhaps you have wisdom beyond this place and can advise me.'

'Tell me your trouble, Sir, and I will if I can.'

'A strange thing it is that a horse from the sea comes to the byre each night. A grey stallion, one of Lir's own, servant of the King of the Sea himself. Each night he tries to cover my mare, but what would we do with any foal he sires, it being neither of the land nor the sea? Do you know of a way that I can dissuade him?'

'Indeed it would be an easy thing. Cut some strands of your mare's mane and scrape some parings from her hooves. Put these above the byre door and you'll be troubled no more.'

The old man thanked him, and soon after made his excuses and went to bed. The stranger spoke to the young woman for the rest of that night and was gone by dawn. Again his seat could not be dried until sprinkled with sand and salt.

That evening, the old man took some scissors to his daughter's hair and then her nails. He placed hair and clippings in a pouch of bladderwrack and nailed them above the door which he barred. Before long the latch lifted, lifted and rattled, rattled again with more force. But the door did not open. Then they heard a laugh, a laugh as wild and as skirling as the cry of a gull.

'The People of the Land have great cunning and if One of the Sea has been bested, it is because last night he opened his mouth too wide.'

In their cottage by the sea, father and daughter never saw hide nor hair of the selkie again.

The Selkie Bride

The farmer rarely had the leisure to walk the strand, but on this evening the hay harvest was in early and there was still daylight to enjoy. He had already walked far and walked even further when he heard the singing. Lovely and otherworldly it was. There she sat, her naked back towards him, and although that was all he could see of her, he knew she was the loveliest woman he ever would see. But was she a woman? Beside her on the rock lay a mottled sealskin. He knew then that she was a selkie, and he would have to be quick.

His steps made no sound on the smooth rocks. Then his hand was on the skin and it was whipped behind his back as he laid the other on her bare shoulder.

'Now that I have your skin, you must come with me.'

It was true. Without it she could not become a seal again and return to her home in the sea. How she pleaded with him to return it, running along naked beside him, begging him to give her back her skin, tugging it under his arm. But his grip was firm and his mind was firmer. He loved her too much to let her go. He didn't love her enough to let her go.

So the selkie became his wife and three times she became a mother. Her husband was good to her in his way, and she loved their children, but oh how she longed for the sea. Whenever she could, she looked for her sealskin, but she never found it. Secretly the man kept changing its hiding place, now atop a rafter in the barn, now beneath the clinker flag on the hearth. Years passed, she never found it and she never stopped looking.

It was harvest time; all the family were glad to be stacking the last stook of oats in the lower field. The selkie woman left her family to finish the work and went inside to start the supper. When they were all seated, the youngest piped up.

'Father, why were you hiding that smelly sealskin in the last stook? Won't it foul the grain?'

She hadn't finished her second question before her mother had leaped up. Her father too leaped from his chair and blocked the doorway. But it was summer and the window was open. One leap and she was on the table, another and she was through it. She was way ahead of him before he cleared the corner of the cottage, running swifter than a swallow down to the lower field. All her family followed. The oat stalks flew, golden arrows in the sunset, as she tore that stook apart. Then there was a grey cloud amongst the gold. There was a swirl of grey like smoke as she swept her sealskin around her shoulders and ran towards the sea. The weight of years of longing was lifted from her as she ran. No one could catch her.

When she reached the shore, the skin was close about her. The selkie did not look back. She plunged into the surf. There across the water rose the head of a great bull seal, her first husband come to meet her. Beside him were the heads of three smaller seals, her first family come to greet her.

Some say that every evening, whether rain or shine, summer or winter, the selkie would return to that part of the strand. As her children ran along the shore, she would throw up brightly coloured shells and fresh caught fish for them. Some said that it was not like that and if ever a boat put out to sea with young people in it, a grey seal would appear. She would swim round about it crying pitifully and then would dive beneath it. The passengers would feel it rocking as she sought to overturn it and take her children with her to the home they had never known, beneath the sea.

Gotham's Eel

Some lucky readers will already know that every country worth its flag has its own distinctive village of fools. Gotham is England's home-grown variety.

The people of Gotham were always up to some clever plan and prided themselves on their inventive schemes. It was nearly spring, and the stalwart inhabitants were coming to the end of their winter rations of salted fish. As though of one mind, the villagers decided to save their last scraps and put them in the village pond so that the various species would swim forth and multiply over the warmer months. Their being placed in the village pond would ensure an easy fishy harvest in the autumn.

Not to be outdone, neighbour after neighbour showed off the by now leathery remains of cod, herring, whiting, haddock and more, before throwing the scraps of the ocean's bounty into the pond. One was embarrassed at having nothing to contribute, having devoured his last kipper the night before, but as it was elver-catching season, he managed to contribute an eel. Perhaps surprised at his stroke of genius, he decided that he wanted this act of generosity to be commemorated. Having heard that physical characteristics could be passed on to the next generation, but being a bachelor, he thought to make a mark on the eel's skin in the spirit of science. But which mark to make? Long deliberation resulted in the shape of the letters 'T' and 'H' being nicked above the beast's eyes, as its donor was named Thomas.

A rota was drawn up to keep watch on the new fishery, lest any were stolen. At last the day came when all were allocated identical fishing tackle and a spot on the bank. The village fishing event began and everyone sat in a circle, the only sound being the occasional whirr of a line being cast. By the end of the day not a single fish had been landed. The villagers agreed that the fish must have caught some of their own cunning whilst captive in their midst. It was therefore decided to trawl the pond and share out the catch. This procedure resulted in the usual collection of unpaired boots, holed saucepans, wedding and engagement rings, and not a single cod, haddock, herring, whiting or more.

But there was something writhing in the net. It was a very large eel with the unmistakable marks 'T' and 'H' on its head, which had grown into the size of a badge. If anyone doubted the identity of the fish THief, here it was, already branded as one. Those initials in themselves were sufficient judge, jury and conviction. The discussion as to its fitting punishment did not last long. A unanimous vote ensured that it was drowned in the river.

Davey Kisses his Catch

Davey was a solitary young man whose one passion was fishing. His temperament, therefore, was well suited to his favourite pastime. He had tried to get a girlfriend in the past, but had just been too shy to get anywhere, so he had given up. It wasn't that the girls didn't like him, he was a handsomer boy than most. They interpreted his long silences as being those of a deep thinker, whereas Davey was just tongue-tied. They thought him gentlemanly as he didn't make a pass at them, whereas he was just terrified. Eventually when they didn't get anywhere with him at all, they decided he was a 'cold fish'.

One day, like many others, found Davey all alone in his boat on the river with his rod and line. When it grew taut he knew that this could be his biggest catch ever. From the way the boat was bucking up and down in the water like an unbroken foal, he knew that not even his big arms could be stretched wide enough to tell his mother how large the fish was. So he thought that he had better bring in the fish itself rather than be disbelieved.

He couldn't understand how the line didn't break with that monster at the other end of it. There was so much splashing as he tried to heave it into the boat that he wondered why the boat didn't sink with all the water she had taken on, or how it was that she hadn't been overturned by the creature's thrashing tail. At last manly strength prevailed and the fish was in the boat, although there was barely room for the two of them.

Out of the water it was strangely quiet, and it looked at Davey with eyes that were soft rather than glassy. After that mighty struggle, the hook had become deeply embedded and Davey was having trouble extricating it. At last he managed, but only by tearing open the side of the fish's great mouth. A stream of blood ran down, and for the first time in his fishing life, the lad felt a pang of pity.

'Kiss me, Davey.'

He heard it distinctly, but there was nobody there who could have spoken. Davey looked carefully along each empty bank. There wasn't so much as a bird in sight after all that commotion.

'Kiss me, Davey.'

The voice was definitely coming from inside the boat. There wasn't room for any other creature with that huge fish in there, and fish don't speak.

'Kiss me better, Davey.'

This time he saw the mouth move, and as it did, more blood trickled down. Davey looked around again. Still nobody. Nobody there, so nobody to see, nobody to see, so nobody to tell. He shut his eyes and kissed the fish right on the wound he had made with the hook.

The first thing his lips told him was that the fish was warm, the next was that the blood tasted just like his own. When he opened his eyes, it seemed to him that he was looking through a veil of water. He saw the fish shimmy off those scales until shell-pink skin appeared. He saw a shake of the head loose a swirl of river-brown hair. He saw those soft eyes slip round to the front of the face, green as reeds. He saw that gashed mouth knit and heal, turn into the curling wave of soft lips.

'Take me to where there's room for two, Davey.'

If people in the village thought there was something fishy about this woman's sudden appearance out of nowhere, they didn't say so. If they mentioned to Davey that she was quite a catch, his reply was his usual slow shy smile. It is certain that they lived happily ever after. Strange to say, but true, all the children born to them, all their children's children and all their descendants, were born with a thin white scar that stretched from the corner of their mouths across to their ears.

The Otter King

King Cormac had four children, but his only son had died as a child. His daughters roamed the realm together as they pleased, a delight to their father and a joy to the people.

It was the custom after Beltane, May Eve, for the king to journey throughout the land in the summer months. The weather being exceptionally fine for the season, and the queen being in failing health, it was decided that for once they would set off earlier. It was not this break with tradition that concerned Cormac, but leaving his girls unattended on May Eve – that unchancy time when the veil between this and the Other World is thin. The day before his departure, he took his troubled thoughts on a walk around the great lake that lay beneath his fort.

In the slanting sunlight he saw a great ring of ripples and wondered what creature could be large enough to make it. When a huge round head appeared in their midst, it seemed for a moment that he was looking at an immense eye on the surface of the water. The head was too large even for a bull seal that occasionally swam upstream into the lake chasing salmon. It was then that Cormac remembered the stories of the Otter King. The monstrous head drew nearer and he knew the tales to be true as king stared at king, blue eyes to black and black back to blue. Then, sinuous as a snake, King Otter threw back his head and yawned. Cormac glimpsed the voracious crimson throat fringed with its dagger-sharp teeth before it dived. On returning to the court, he summoned his daughters and forbade them ever to swim in the lake.

Spring had come early and was warmer than some summers.

The girls soon tired of their usual games – playing hopscotch backwards over lark's nests, swapping gull's eggs on the sea cliffs and rolling cuckoo's eggs down weasel's burrows. Beltane dawned already hot; the sky stretched tight with the heat of August. Copper clouds thickened and even the cuckoos fell silent. How Cormac's daughters longed to swim. They remembered their father's command, but what was the harm in swimming where they had swum so often before? When it was dark, they slipped away without telling the servants where they were going.

As they reached the centre of the lake, the storm broke and the water was instantly churned into waves that slapped at them from all directions. Tiring fast, they struck out for the shore that they could now only see in the lightning flashes. The youngest sister was not strong enough to keep up and became separated from her sisters. For a moment she was reassured by the sensation of a body swimming alongside her, but suddenly there came a foetid smell of fish as she felt the back of her neck being stabbed by sharp rows like a huge and savage comb. Still clasping her neck, an immense weight was bearing her down beneath the surface, where she felt her body pierced as if by a blade of fire. Then she was pushed from below until she surfaced. She was alone, floating on the lake, with the last of the storm fleeing from the gentle dawn of May's first morning.

How relieved was the search party to see her walking towards them along the shore. With no harm done, it was easy to reach an unspoken agreement not to mention anything about the episode. Later that day she noticed untimely blood between her thighs, but as time passed the expected bleeding never came. Summer passed into autumn and Cormac returned to celebrate the feast of Samhain, Halloween. News of the death of the queen had preceded him and the girls were exceptionally eager to greet their father. The court rejoiced to receive him and all smiled as he embraced his daughters, but when the youngest ran to him she received a slap that sent her reeling. Shocked and confused, she reached towards him again and was struck to the ground.

'When last I saw you, you were a maid. Now I am looking at a mother. What man have you been with when my back was turned?'

She knew not to rise or face her father in his anger. Kneeling before him, she told of her swim in the lake, of that overwhelming body, of that instant blood that did not return with the months' passing. The king was looking down at the nape of her neck where her hair had parted. He saw a double row of crimson marks and remembered the Otter King. Pity and forgiveness raised her eyes to his. Blue looked into blue.

'The first blow was for disobeying your father and the second for disobeying your king.' And no more was said of it, unless it was amongst the servants who never risked being heard referring to the 'Cuckoo Prince' when the boy was born.

Cormac was pleased to have an heir and treated his grandson like his own son so that in time many forgot the truth of it. Even as a baby it was said that he was always wakeful. The servants remembered the old tales that told how water creatures can never sleep on land. Out of their element they are always restless – just as tides and currents are never still – but with the movement of water around them they can be at peace. Those servants wisely only mentioned this amongst themselves.

Conn grew faster and braver than most – apart from a fear of dogs, strange in a prince. If unable to avoid being close to one, he could not restrain the snarl that bared his pointed teeth. His huge dark eyes would become fixed as every dog would growl and snap and have to be whipped away.

One day before he was half grown, he was walking with his grandfather when the ageing king stumbled.

'You're getting too old to rule. Who would respect a feeble king? Better by far to pass the kingship to me before there is trouble.'

Cormac was shocked to hear this but put it down to the tactlessness of the young. Soon similar comments followed and the king was hurt and troubled by this unkindness. A year after that Conn strode down the feasting hall. His high-pitched whistling voice could be heard above the clamour of the dogs, who had become a pack baying their challenge.

'This is your last chance, old man, give me the kingship or have it taken from you by force!'

The king rose. How had it come to pass that this boy was already taller than the man? Blue stared at black and black stared back.

'You've had your warning, old man.'

The youth strode away and there were plenty of courtiers who would have released their dogs at the slightest sign from the king, but it did not come.

Conn made his way to a distant part of the country where none knew of his secret nickname 'the Cuckoo Prince'. There he asked to be taken into the service of Finn Mac Cumhaill, the greatest warrior in Ireland. Strangely he showed no fear of Finn's dogs, nor they any animosity to him. This was because they too had other worldly blood (but how that happened is another story) and something in all of them recognised each other. So it was that Finn had no suspicion of this stranger, especially when he said that he was King Cormac's heir. When Finn asked what the boy wanted for his wages, he was told that Conn would only claim them if he did everything that Finn reasonably asked for at the instant he asked it. If he fulfilled those conditions for a year and a day, Finn was to give him anything he requested. Finn, fair and trusting as his name and reputation, didn't realise what an unchancy bargain had been struck.

Meanwhile, King Cormac tried to take his mind off his sorrows by hunting in the forests. One day he paused to rest by a lonely blacksmith's forge. Watching him at work, he was reminded of how smiths were gifted beyond the powers of ordinary men because of the sacred calling of their craft. The smith also had three daughters and the king, now that his heir had become his enemy, thought for the first time to marry again. Grainne, the youngest, was the only one not spoken for and they were soon married. Before long her swelling belly was soothing the hurt caused by his grandson.

'Perhaps I will have a true heir to my realm,' thought the king.

Conn's faultless service of a year and a day was nearly over when a druid approached Finn and warned him about his foolish bargain. He had divined that no good would come of it and that the land itself would be in peril. Finn, Ireland's appointed guardian, grew fearful and asked the druid what he should do. The druid told him that he must find a way to prevent Conn from fulfilling his side of the agreement.

Finn decided that he would order Conn to sleep outside his tent on the last night of his service, whilst he would have his own companions keeping watch inside with him. They would take it in turns to rouse Finn every hour, at which he would command the youth to bring him some object, hoping that the lad's drowsiness would cause him to delay. This was done, but nobody knew that Conn's father was the Otter King, and that he had inherited the water creature's sleeplessness. The ruse was therefore useless as Conn carried out each order without delay. Finn could not deny him his wages and dreaded what they might be. The request to make war on King Cormac was beyond Finn's worst imaginings, but he was honour-bound to keep his side of the bargain.

Finn's war host was duly gathered and Cormac knew that he would lose, as did all who fought that mighty band. He sent Grainne back to her father to be safe, giving orders that her father should use his art to fashion the baby a belt of gold with a plaque on which was written the child's name and parentage. As was feared, Cormac died in that battle and his grandson became King Conn.

The new king was as predatory and voracious as his true father and all hated him. The land itself rebelled against his cruelty – crops withered and even the trees grew twisted. Far from the court in the smithy by the forest, Grainne knew that her birthing time had come. She took a woman to help her and they went into the forest where the child could be born secretly. As soon as the boy was in this world, Grainne told the woman to fit the gold belt about him. No sooner was this done, than a she-wolf appeared from the trees and stole the baby away.

Years later, a hunting party came to that part of the forest and saw the wolf playing with the boy along with her own cubs. The boy was captured, which probably saved his life, as that belt was by now sinking into his flesh as though to cut him in two. When they removed the belt, they realised who he was and decided to take him to a king in another part of the country. Knowing that the boy's life would be in danger if Conn got to hear of him, and being childless, King MacGillon was happy to adopt him.

As he grew, the young prince excelled at every task his masters set him and was as fearless, persistent and cunning as any wolf. The other boys were jealous when yet again he beat them at a game and they began to taunt him, calling him 'Son of a Wolf'. He was surprised when his tutor didn't reprimand them, and his cunning told him that there was something behind this. Then he went to the king and demanded to know why he was being called 'Son of a Wolf'.

The king told him the story of how he was found and showed him the belt.

'This is not the end of the story, it is the beginning,' said the prince, and left to find King Cormac's court.

On he went through the forest with his tireless loping stride. When he reached its furthest edge, he saw an old man in a solitary house. He asked where King Cormac's court was and the old man began to cry, telling the lad how he and everyone had loved the old king and how they suffered under the new. It was too late to travel on that night, so the prince stayed with the old man and his daughter. Getting ready for sleep, he stretched and yawned and the woman saw the belt on him and wept. She explained how she recognised it and mother, son and grandfather embraced each other for the first time.

The following day he went to what was now King Conn's court. Nobody made him welcome as hospitality demanded, so he helped himself to food in the kitchen. When the servants remonstrated, he told them he would be working there for a while – what task did they have for him? They told him that King Conn always had need of a storyteller to while away the long nights – they didn't mention that the king never slept, was never satisfied with the stories he heard, and always beheaded the storyteller in the morning for falling asleep before him.

When he was taken to Conn, he was commanded to tell the best stories he knew. With relentless stamina he told tale after tale all night long. In the morning the king was astonished and said that all the stories the lad told were the best he had ever heard.

'But you can't have heard them all, you must have fallen asleep,' said the boy.

'I heard them all and I never sleep, would that I could,' said the king.

'If you never sleep, you must have a touch of the otter in you,' said the boy, who of course knew the old stories.

'Don't you let me hear you say that again,' threatened the king. 'Now tell me more tales.'

Then: 'Those were even better than before. How do you do it?'

'Indeed, how do *you* do it,' said the boy. 'Never falling asleep even for a moment – you must be at least half otter!'

'I warned you,' cried the king and leaped for his sword.

'Rather than point your sword at me, you should point it at your own mother's throat and ask her the manner of your begetting. I am not the only storyteller here.'

Conn ran to his mother's chamber, pressed her into the bed with the weight of his body and let her feel the point of his sword on the back of her neck.

'Now tell me who my father is,' and she did.

Then Conn returned to the boy. 'Is there as much truth in all the tales you tell?'

'If you want more, I can tell you how you can fall asleep at last.'

King Conn heard how he should take a boat and drop anchor in the middle of the lake and how he was to get a great chain, attaching it to the boat and fastening it to trees on opposite sides of the shore. He was to place his bed in the middle of the boat, and there at last, with the rocking of the water, he would sleep.

This was done and Conn slept for three days and three nights. But before the third night was quite over, a great dark shape arose from the water. The Otter King silently swarmed along the chain and into the boat. There he found the rival male in his realm and dragged him by the back of the neck into the depths. Next day the servants found his body on one side of the lake and his head on the other.

The Little Crabfish

Reproduced with kind permission from Yvette Staelen's Somerset Sisters *CD.*

Well there was a little man and he had a little wife
And he loved his dear as he loved his life.
Well his wife's with child and she's fallen sick
And all that she wants is a little crabfish.

Well he's arose and put on his clothes
Down to the seaside he followed his nose,
'Oh Fisherman, Oh Fisherman, can you tell to me
Have you got a little crabfish you can sell to me?'

'Oh yes sir, yes sir, one two, three
The best in the basket, I shall sell to thee.'
So he took this little crabfish, he took it by the horn,
He's slung it o'er his back and he's toddled off home.

Ah but when he got it home he couldn't find a dish
So into the chamber pot he threw the crabfish.
Early the next morning, his wife she arose
And felt beneath the bed for to use the so-and-so.

Well she's got down and she began to squat
The crabfish got her by the you-know-what.
So loudly she did scream and so loudly she did grunt
The Devil's in the pot and he's got me by the … front!

'Oh Wife, dearest Wife, you must be going mad,
You can't tell the Devil from an old sea crab.
Oh if it be a sea crab or fish of any kind
It'll let go its hold if you blow it from behind.'

Well he's got down, he's lifted up her clothes
The crab put out a pincer and caught him by the nose.
'Oh I curse the very hour that I brought the thing hither
It's joined me nose and me wife's tail together!'

So you'd better take a look before you take a squat,
make sure there's nothing swimming in the old pee pot.

A Crabby Curiosity

In the days when few could afford to travel, the working life of those who ploughed the land or those who harvested the sea were often a mystery to farmer or fisher. It was therefore easy for antipathy or mockery to flourish between farming and fisherfolk.

A fisherman had caught the largest crab that he had ever seen. Its shell was easily as wide as the log he used to split driftwood into kindling, and he knew that it would fetch a good price on the fish stall. His largest basket was barely enough to accommodate it and when he carried it onto the quay, he weighted the lid down with a stone. However, being unused to crabs of that size, he underestimated its strength. Unnoticed, the crab managed to lever itself out of its basket and scrambled off. Perhaps it was a sense of adventure rather than a yearning for safety that drew it away from its watery home, for it made its way overland to pastures new.

At last it reached a field where the hay harvest was taking place. Hay rakes were thrown down in astonishment, then rapidly taken up again in horror. What was this monster that had appeared in their midst? The bravest of the farmhands attempted to corral the beast with their tools. They had encountered animals that reared, rolled, bit, scratched and bucked, but never encountered an animal that moved sideways before. A strange dance was played out as the monster scuttled sideways and they tried to anticipate its next move whilst accommodating the width of their rakes.

Transfixed, the good workers of the land tried to take in this terrifying apparition. Now that they had caught they-knew-not-what, what were they to do with it? It was clearly too dangerous to let it loose. At last someone suggested that they consult their oldest and wisest and this was agreed to with great relief.

Oldest and Wisest was so old that he had long since been referred to by this title rather than by his name. He was so old that he hardly ever moved or opened his eyes unless it was to drink rum or smoke tobacco, and these he managed to do more often than not without bothering to open them. The assembled heroes realised that in spite of these habits, it would be easier to bring him to the monster than vice versa. One of them was dispatched to rouse the old fellow and fetch him in a wheelbarrow.

All stood firm as they waited, and at last the squeaking of an ancient wheelbarrow could be heard. When it came into sight, the heroes could see that its incumbent still had his eyes shut.

How then could he witness and pronounce on the monster in their midst? A plan was rapidly formed. Pipes were lit and the aromatic fumes of tobacco were wafted at Oldest and Wisest from different directions. At last, nobody having placed a pipe in his mouth, he had to open his eyes to see the source of the bounty of which he was being deprived. The bravest of the heroes was waving a pipe above the monster to draw the old man's attention to it. Perhaps it was these movements that caused the crab to respond by rearing up and trying to grab the pipe with its fearsome pincers.

'Inseck! Inseck!' cried the old man, more animated than anyone could remember seeing him. 'That inseck be worse poison than Solomon's scorpion! Wheel I round, wheel I round. Take me back afore my body bloats like drowned badger and my pinkies turn dark as bluebottle. Wheel I round, wheel I round!'

The farmhands, never before hearing such a long speech from him, were shocked into silence. However, the mention of Solomon confirmed his authority in the knowledge department. The handles of the wheelbarrow were seized again and just as it was about to set a course for home, the fisherman appeared looking for his lost catch. Now all were near paralysed with shock as they saw him lift the monster from behind and shove it into a basket, securing the lid firmly.

The fisherman looked around at the open mouths and the staring eyes, but it was the wheelbarrow, paused in flight, that caught his attention.

'She would cut along a lot faster if you put a sail on her,' he suggested.

This incident was commemorated for many years in a local pub's name: The Crab and Rake. The pub sign was said to at first have depicted a crab brandishing a rake. Legend has it that the landlubbers objected to this falsehood and changed the sign to that of a crab trapped between two rakes as if caught in a gin trap.

Oldest of the Old, Wisest of the Wise

King Arthur had agreed to help his cousin gain the hand of Olwen, who was the daughter of an evil giant. Her father was a murderous brute who had already killed all his nephews but one, and he wasn't going to let his daughter go easily. He set her suitor and his companions a series of impossible tasks, which they undertook together.

The first of these was to find a youth, Mabon, who although born of a divine mother had been stolen from her when he was only three days old. Nobody knew who had stolen him or where he was hidden. It was decided to consult with the oldest beings of all – certain ancient animals – as they were most likely to have heard about or remembered what had happened so very long ago. Arthur entrusted Gwrhyr to take charge of this quest as he could speak the language of all the beasts and the birds.

The companions journeyed until they found the most ancient of blackbirds.

'Most venerable Blackbird, can you tell us anything about Mabon who was stolen from his mother when only three days old?'

'It is true that I am old. When I first came to this place as a young bird, I perched on a smith's anvil that I found here. Each evening I wiped my beak on it and now it has been worn down to the size of a hazelnut. It is true that I am the oldest of my kind, and it is true that I should help any who are sent by King Arthur, but may God strike me if I am able to tell you anything about the one you seek. All I can do is to take you to a creature even older than myself, in case he is the wiser.'

With that the companions followed the most ancient of blackbirds until they came to an old stag.

'Most venerable Stag, can you tell us anything about Mabon who was stolen from his mother when only three days old?'

'When I first came to this place, I was so young that there was only one tine on each of my antlers. From this ground there sprouted but a single oak sapling. Since then I have seen it turn into a mighty oak tree, growing its own antlers of a hundred boughs, with countless branches of tines upon them. I have watched that tree dying until it became that tree stump you see before you, and in all that time I have heard nothing of the one you seek. But as you have been sent by King Arthur, it is the least I can do to help your quest. I am old, but there is another who was made by the Creator before myself.'

With that the companions followed the most ancient of stags until they came to an old owl.

'Most venerable Owl, can you tell us anything about Mabon who was stolen from his mother when only three days old?'

'If I knew anything, I would tell you. When I first came to this valley there grew a great wood. A race of men arrived and cut down every tree. Since then it has grown up again and been cut down, and grown once more. This is the third of its kind that you see now. And as for myself, I am so old that my wings are as the stumps of that felled forest. In all that time I have heard nothing of the one you seek, but I will be a guide to King Arthur's messengers and take you to the oldest creature in the world – the oldest and the one who lives the furthest.'

With that the companions followed the most ancient of owls until they came to an old eagle.

'Most venerable Eagle, can you tell us anything about Mabon who was stolen from his mother when only three days old?'

'When I was first here, I perched on a stone that was so high that I would peck at the stars from it. Since then it has been worn away until it is only as high as the span of your hand. From that day to this day, I have heard nothing of the one you seek, except for one occasion when I went to hunt in a distant lake. I sank my talons into the back of a great salmon, knowing that he would be enough to feed me for many a day, so huge a fish was he. But he was so mighty a creature, that instead of my rising with him from the lake, it was he who dragged me down into its depths. I only got away with great difficulty and so it was that I summoned all my kind to make war on him. However, he sent messengers to make peace with me and after this he returned, asking me to use my talons to take out no less than fifty tridents that had been hurled at him throughout his life. If he doesn't know the one you seek, then I don't know who does. As you are sent from King Arthur, I will take you to him.'

With that the companions followed the most ancient of eagles until they came to an old salmon.

'Most venerable Salmon, can you tell us anything about Mabon who was stolen from his mother when only three days old?'

The salmon, oldest of the old and wisest of the wise, then told the companions of a weeping and wailing he heard each time he followed the tide upstream in the River Severn. At the next tide the great fish took two of the companions on his back to a tower that was almost encircled by the river. There they heard those lamentations and learned that they were the cries made by Mabon himself who had been taken prisoner.

The great salmon took his passengers back to the others and King Arthur was summoned. With all the men-at-arms in Britain he mounted an assault on the tower. Meanwhile, with the next rising tide, the salmon swam back to the tower with Sir Kay and Sir Bedivere on his back. With King Arthur and his force providing a distraction, Sir Kay and Sir Bedivere broke into the back of the tower and rescued Mabon. Oldest of the old, wisest of the wise, the salmon carried all three downstream to safety.

Creeping, Crawling
and Scuttling

How the Birds Helped Hedgehog

The Creator was busy making animals out of clay, shaping them perfectly, one by one, and then breathing life into them so that they could run, swim or fly away. When it came to Hedgehog's turn, he was getting impatient and started wiggling around in God's hands before he was quite ready. Like a forbearing mother, God sighed at the little creature's impatience. But that was enough to give life to him and Hedgehog scuttled away without any outer covering except for his bare skin. Apart from looking very odd alongside all the feathered and furred companions of the woods, Hedgehog felt most uncomfortable. Bitten by mosquitoes, pricked by brambles and stung by nettles, he got sunburned on hot days and shivered in every breeze. This put him in a permanent bad temper and he grunted and groaned all day long, complaining to any animal he came across.

Next time the Creator visited this part of the world, it was to be met by a disgruntled reception committee. Somewhat startled not to receive the usual gratitude and praise, God instead had to listen to all their grievances about having Hedgehog as their neighbour. A remedy was needed, and the Creator generously decreed that Hedgehog could choose any covering from any of the animals in the forest, and it would be granted him. All were happy with this arrangement.

Hedgehog trotted off to view the options and make his decision. It was surprisingly difficult given the variety, and given how hard he was to please. There was something wrong with all the fur he saw: too heavy; too light; too warm; too sparse; too dull; too dark; too smooth; too rough and so it went on. As he scuttled alongside a stream, he thought for a moment of asking for fish scales as they gleamed so enticingly. However, he soon changed his mind when he remembered coming across a dead fish out of water and what it smelled like. Then Jay swooped across his path and Hedgehog stopped. Feathers – of course! Warm in winter, cool in summer, never too heavy, could be worn sleek or fluffy.

'The perfect choice, Hedgehog, though I say it Myself,' he could almost hear the Creator whispering.

Was it a prayer, was it a wish? He was just about to voice his decision when he paused. Colourful though Jay was, there were other birds who were more so. How to choose, whom to choose? But did he have to? 'Any covering from any of the animals …' was what had been said. Maybe he could get away with requesting the most colourful feathers from all of the most colourful birds. It was worth a try. He clasped his little scrabbling paws together (that was the praying bit), screwed his little piggy eyes tight shut (that was the wishing bit) and squeaked what he wanted.

There was a whirring and a rustling and when he opened his eyes he was surrounded by the brightest of the birds, each with colourful feathers in their beaks. Blue Tit stabbed him with blue and yellow feathers, Woodpecker with green and red, Woodpigeon with iridescent mauve, Kingfisher with turquoise and orange, and so it went on. Yes, it pierced and pricked, like being stuck in a bramble patch, but it was worth it. When all their offerings had been made, Hedgehog was the most glorious fluffy ball of brilliant colours. All breathed a sigh of relief.

But not for long. Hedgehog's behaviour did not improve and he was even harder to live with than before. Now that he was the most beautiful animal in the forest, he expected special treatment, even demanding that others fetch and carry for him. All the birds who had given him feathers were furious. The Creator could hear the next reception committee long before he could see it, loud as it was with its cacophony of indignant squaws and screeches. Promising to do something soon, Divine Power hastened the approach of autumn.

Like many in the forest, Hedgehog made ready for his hibernation. This time, however, he evicted an entire family of rabbits from their burrow and bullied another family of squirrels into filling it with the softest and driest of fallen leaves. As he slept that long winter sleep, he had a most uncomfortable dream in which he was being turned inside out. It was the kind of unpleasant dream from which one tries to awaken oneself, but as hibernation lasts for months, he was unable to.

At last spring came and Hedgehog scuttled off to find his first breakfast of the year. He spied a curious animal in a puddle that lay across his path.

'If I looked as strange as you, I would stay at home until dark. And exactly how long are you going to keep me standing here before you move out of my way?'

But the creature didn't move out of the way because it was his own reflection. It was like a bad dream come true. It *was* a bad dream come true. Hedgehog had been turned inside out and the glorious coloured feathers were now on the inside with their quills on the outside. That is why when we see Hedgehog today we see him covered in spikes, and with those feathers on the inside, tickling him wherever he goes, he scuttles around even faster than before.

Robert the Bruce's Spider

The lesson well could trace,
Which even 'he who runs may read,'
That Perseverance gains its meed,
And Patience wins the race.

Bernard Barton

Robert the Bruce, King of Scotland, had been defeated in battle by the English. He became a fugitive and hid from his enemies in a cave. There he despaired, frustrated at this enforced inactivity when his country needed him, and bored to distraction as, with the passing months, his refuge became more and more like a prison.

In the midst of his misery, he noticed something shining at the mouth of the cave. It was a single strand of gossamer – a spider was trying to attach the first thread of a web. Time and time again, the breeze broke the thread. Time and time again the spider started anew at its task, undaunted. At last the anchor thread was in place and Robert watched as the little creature spun a perfect web. He took this to be a lesson in perseverance, and waited patiently for his moment to come. It did, years later at the Battle of Bannockburn, when his forces defeated the English army against impossible odds.

This was not the only time a spider had saved a fugitive. Many centuries before, an early Christian convert was fleeing from his persecutors. He hid in a cave, with the pursuit already searching the area for him. Spiders began spinning cobwebs with which they cloaked the entrance to the cave. It was an obvious place to hide in, and an obvious place to search.

When the soldiers reached the mouth of the cave, one of them pointed out the thick covering of webs. As they were intact, it appeared that nothing had gone in or out for some time, and his hiding place was not disturbed.

How Spider Became Wolf

There was an old woman who swallowed a spider
That wriggled and wriggled and tickled inside her.
She swallowed the spider to catch the fly,
I don't know why she swallowed a fly, perhaps she'll die!
There was an old woman who swallowed a bird,
Have you heard? She swallowed a bird!
She swallowed the bird to catch the spider
That wriggled and wriggled and tickled inside her.

Spider couldn't understand why most people were terrified of her when it was she who was frightened of almost every other living creature. She lurked in dark corners, knowing that even timid little Mouse would eat her if given a chance. Hiding from everyone, she waited for flies to be caught in her web. Sometimes, before this happened, she heard them buzzing to each other about the goings-on in the village and beyond.

That is how she knew that in the village lived an old woman reputed to have magical powers. It was even said that she had turned a boy into a toad for stealing apples. This had given Spider food for thought, and she wished that she dared approach the woman and ask to be turned into a different kind of animal. The one thing that prevented her from doing this was the fear that the witch would want to keep her just as she was, for use in one of her spells.

In time, Spider heard the flies buzzing about a newcomer to the abbey beyond the village. This was a holy man who spent most of his time praying and meditating on the gospels. It was said that he was so holy that he too had special powers. Once he had turned a flock of pigeons, gorging on a poor farmer's wheat crop, into a flock of butterflies. With a flick of holy water, he had transformed a rabid dog into a suckling pig. Spider came up with a plan.

She caught Fly in her web, but didn't kill it. She promised to spare its life if it found out from its friends the way to where the holy man lived. This it managed to do, and asked Spider to keep her side of the bargain.

'Not yet, my little friend. First we are going on a journey.'

Spider tied a length of web to one of Fly's legs. Holding fast to the loose end, she skilfully unpicked her web from its body until it could fly freely except for its tether.

'Let's go!' And off they went.

It was a long journey, but at last they reached the holy man's cell and Spider released Fly. There was not even a twitch as she crawled over the monk's hands, climbed the slope of his neck, and whispered into his ear.

'Holy Man, Holy Man, they say that you have magical powers, that you help the weak, that you can work miracles. If that's true, please do something for me! I am too frightened to come out into the light because there are so many animals who would eat me. All my relatives have been eaten by birds – except for my husbands, that is – please would you turn me into a bird?'

No sooner had she finished speaking, then six of her eight legs had become two wings and all those spiky hairs on them had become feathers. Eight eyes had become two, pincer jaws were now a beak, and most glorious of all, feathered wings stretched, fluttered and flew. It was such a joy to be a bird. Bird sang and swooped, dipped and darted until she was tired. She hopped down from a branch to have a dust bath. Preening beneath her wings, she nearly didn't notice that new shadow. Somehow it wasn't attached to the ground any more, somehow its menace was hurtling towards her. As the shadow pounced, Bird took off, leaving some feathers in the cat's paws. A lucky escape, Bird trembled up on the branch.

As soon as she dared, Bird flew back to the monk, and in through the cell's open window.

'Holy Man, Holy Man, I don't want to be a bird anymore. Couldn't you turn me into a cat?'

What a comfort to feel those ruffled feathers turn into velvety fur. How thrilling to stretch those legs, spring coiled, dagger finished. Every pinch of pride was in that raised and wafting tail, as Cat prowled back to where Bird had nearly been caught. How drowsy a pleasure to lie full length, purring in the sun-warmed dust. Until the pack of dogs that roamed the grounds picked up her scent. They were a snarling mass upon her, too many legs churning to know which ones to dart through. A paw-full of dagger slashes on the most eager muzzle cleared the way. A desperate dash and skitter up the trunk, and teeth snapped on a mouthful of fur.

Cat gripped the branch, swearing at the barking pack below. They were long gone before she could persuade her claws to let go. As soon as she dared, Cat slunk back to the monk, and in through the open door of his cell.

'Holy Man, Holy Man, I don't want to be a cat any more. Can't you turn me into a dog?'

How powerful it was to feel those legs lengthening, tightening with latent speed. How exciting to feel that nose extending, drinking in that bewildering mix of smells. Dog trotted off towards the scent and sound of the pack, rolled in the dust and showed a submissive belly in a plea to be accepted. What fun it was to scratch fleas and leave liquid messages on tree trunks. Best of all, how cool it was to be in a gang. The day dipped towards night, and the rest of the pack knew to be inside during the hours of darkness. They knew the comfort of scraps around a warm hearth, the safety of fire and human company.

Dog hadn't been a dog for long enough to know these. There was still a world of scents to explore, but he wasn't alone in this as Wolf sniffed hungrily at the smell of evening cooking. Wolf padded out of the forest, crept closer for a circuit of the sheep pens, for any other opportunity. Then he smelled his age-old enemy – Dog – and Dog was close. There was a frantic rolling in the dirt with Wolf snapping to gain a throat hold and a fierce twisting as Dog broke away. Those legs knew a speed they had never known as Wolf gave chase. Dog's howls brought people to doors and Wolf was seen off. Dog spent the rest of the night twitching in fear on some grateful stranger's floor, one who believed that he had guarded them from the wolf.

Next day, Dog trotted back to the monk and pushed open the door of his cell.

'Holy Man, Holy Man, I don't want to be a dog any more. Why don't you turn me into a wolf?'

Hearing stretched beyond distance. There seemed no limit to that surge of strength. How to contain the urge to run and run forever? But there was also an unease, the certain sense of danger that comes with being in the wrong place. Already Wolf could hear the dog pack snuffling at his scent, whimpering excitedly as they quested for its source. But inside Wolf, hunger gnawed. Food was nearer than the enemy. Hunger won against fear and Wolf sprang upon the Holy Man. As the very tip of Wolf's fang touched the monk's throat, there was no wolf to be seen in that cell. The only creature moving was a spider that scurried down his robe and into the darkest corner, where she started to spin her web.

The holy man came out of his meditative trance and reached for the book he was illuminating. To his dismay, he noticed what seemed to be an ink blot on the page. Peering closer, he realised that it was a dead fly, gossamer tied in a spider's web. When Spider had released her prisoner, a puff of breeze had wrapped the loose thread around Fly, and he had never regained his freedom. The monk sighed, perhaps with relief that his copy had not been spoiled, perhaps with pity at the tiny corpse. As his breath touched it, the tiny legs stirred and then moved of their own accord. Gently, the monk peeled away Spider's single thread. There was a buzzing and Fly was gone, through the open window and into the light.

Mischievous Moles and Mole-Catchers

True as twig grows from branch and branch grows from bough
Here's how a two-legged mole fell foul of a plough –
Mole-catcher Mick was behind this tall tale
He'll tell you himself for a pint of fine ale.

Mole-catcher by night and mole-catcher by day
When ploughboy a visit to wifey would pay.
With sun or moon shining how they did play
Sporting upstairs and downstairs with hubby away.

Mole-catcher Mick was growing suspicious
And laid his plan so cunning malicious,
He hid in the pigpen and didn't wait long
When along came the ploughboy, lusty with song.

He knocked on the door and Mick heard him say,
'Where is your hubby, my darling, I pray?'
'He's off after moles, too far for to hear.'
Neither did know that hubby was near.

So busy were they at their fun and their frolicks
Ploughboy was mazed at *three* hands round his bollocks!
As he squeezed tighter, hubby did smile,
'I've not seen a two-legged mole this long while!'

'I'll have you pay rent for working this ground,
Your ploughing will cost you the best of ten pounds.'
The ploughboy replied, 'A fair sum I don't mind,
As it works out at about one penny a time.'

So all you ploughboys take care who you snatch
And don't become one of the mole-catcher's catch,
For if you are caught with the mole-catcher's wife
You'll risk your plough tackle for the rest of your life.

This was the song that Micky the Mole often sang whilst seated at his campfire, waiting for a summons to his next job.

Micky was the best mole-catcher in the country, and he could afford to pick and choose his clients. At last came an offer he couldn't refuse, from a wealthy estate with a new owner. The young lord had done everything he could to defy Nature and tidy up his tiny corner of the world. Ancient trees had been felled, a river had been diverted and most of the estate had been converted into green sward, predictable and unvaried as far as the eye could see.

Just as he had shaped all to his satisfaction, an army of moles had made their presence known. The lord's view was blighted by unsightly molehills wherever he looked and he was furious. Orders were given to the head gardener to get rid of the moles, and the massacre began. Eventually it seemed that molekind had been conquered. All was green and smooth once more, with every blade of grass the same height as its neighbour and all pointing in the same direction.

The next day an enormous molehill appeared, the size of a kennel. This was followed by several more and their numbers kept increasing.

'That be the King of the Moles, Sir,' said the head gardener with a grin. 'King of the Moles have come on account of his people being in trouble. There's only one mortal can get rid of he, Sir, and that be Micky the Mole.'

So it was that Micky the Mole had graciously accepted the summons and had been promised a bag of gold equal to the King of the Mole's weight if he captured him alive. All this had been accomplished, and as the lord glared malevolently at the creature who was the size of a calf, he pronounced:

'Now take him away and put him to the most painful and lingering death you can think of, as fit punishment for causing me so much trouble. Then come back and tell me how you did it, and I'll give you another bag of gold.'

The King of the Moles was dragged away in his cage, and before long, Micky the Mole was back.

'Well? How did he die?'

'It happened like this, Sir: I thought of roasting him slowly, turning him on a spit. But then I thought that would be too quick a death. I thought of drowning him in the river, where the tide rises slowly. But then I thought it too gentle a death. I thought of poisoning him. But then I thought it too sweet a death. So in the end, I buried him alive!'

'Capital my good man, capital!' The delighted lord gave Micky the Mole another bag of gold and he and his accomplice lived to enjoy many another day.

The Grateful Ants

King Arthur and his companions had been helping his cousin to win the hand of the giant's daughter. Olwen's father, huge, powerful and cunning, had set her suitor a seemingly endless list of impossible tasks. After they had accomplished many of these, the companions dispersed for a time.

Gwythyr, who knew the languages of all the animals, was riding alone. His horse was jumpy with the scent of smoke on the horizon. Some part of the heath must be ablaze as it often was at that time of year. Then he heard a sound that brought such dismay and sorrow for all it was tiny and piercing. He didn't want to linger, the smoke was growing thicker, the crackle of approaching flames drowning out that distressing sound. Nevertheless, he dismounted and looked for its source. To his surprise it came from an ant heap – he had heard the panic-stricken calls of its inhabitants.

'Get down, get down below ground,' he called, and the ants obeyed.

When he could no longer see a single one of them scuttling on the mound's surface, he drew his sword. With one sweep he sliced off its top, levelling it to the ground. There was just time for him to remount and gallop beyond the reach of the fire. The flames unfurled and crackled up every twig and branch. Driven by the stiff wind, the fire moved so swiftly along the earth, that although scorched, nothing at ground level burned. Reduced in height, the ant's nest did not catch alight, and none were harmed. Gwythyr looked back to see if the ants had survived. Faintly he heard their queen call to him: 'God's blessing on you for this good deed. God's blessing go with you and ours with it. When you need to find that which no man can find, we will find it for you.'

The giant had demanded that every seed of flax from a particular place be gathered up and placed before him. They amounted to countless thousands, and it was these ants that piled them up in front of the giant. However, with his magical powers, he was nevertheless able to count them all and noticed that one of them was missing. The companions were about to fail in this task, when just in time, a lame ant hobbled up, bearing the missing seed. Were it not for the help repaid by a grateful army of ants, King Arthur and his companions would have failed in their quest.

A Rick of Rats

It is well known that rats have the ability to predict disasters, especially at sea. They have been known to leap onto any kind of flotsam to get away from ships that showed no signs of disrepair but which foundered shortly afterwards. Every farm has its fair share of rats, and this tale was told to the author by an elderly woman brought up on a remote farm.

She and her brother had been forbidden to play in the hayrick – a favourite place for all rural children for games of hide and seek. They had repeatedly been told that it wasn't safe, and supposed that this was because the bales might fall on them. Knowing that their agility would be proof against any such mishap, the warnings were ignored.

One fine September evening they sneaked off to play amongst the great bales of hay that were piled under a huge open barn. This time, before they were even close, they stopped. In the slanting evening light they could see what appeared to be smoke creeping along the ground towards them like an oily dark tide. They couldn't understand why it hadn't risen into the air or why there was no accompanying smell. They stood still as stones with surprise, and that is what probably saved their lives.

That creeping tide of smoke was an army of rats on the march, leaving the hayrick all at once. It swept up to the children, swarming over anything and everything in its path. By now it was so close that the children could see the thousands of rats scuttling towards them at top speed. When they reached any obstacle, the rats stacked themselves up, using each other like steps and ladders. As they stood, petrified, that army scrabbled and scuttled and squeaked their way over them like they were two fence posts. They didn't know how long they stood there before the last of the rats had disappeared and they dared to move at last.

Fear of the consequences of disobeying their parents prevented them from describing their horrific experience that evening. The next day, that hayrick burst into flames. The rats must have sensed its temperature increasing and saved themselves. It was then that the children plucked up the courage to tell their parents what they had experienced. They could have been punished for disobeying. They could have been punished for not telling what had happened beforehand, thus giving their parents a chance to save the hay harvest. Instead they watched them grow pale as they listened. Their mother wept with relief as she said, 'If you had so much as stirred a foot those varmints would have eaten you alive. In those numbers, they would have pulled you down and stripped every mouthful of flesh from your bones. It's happened before to beasts in the field that have tried to outrun a swarm of rats, and there's no creature that can.'

Missy Mouse Marries the Moon

Mr and Mrs Mouse could look forward to having at least 120 children in their happy marriage as long as the farm cat didn't eat them first. However, in their most recent litter, they were quite sure that one of the babies was extra special. Amongst all the babies born to them, or indeed to any other mouse family in the whole country, it was clear to the adoring parents that this particular mouselet was destined for great things. Before she was even covered with fur, which her parents knew would be radiantly beautiful, they were out and about arranging for the kind of exalted marriage beyond the dreams of any whiskered creature.

Her luminous beauty meant that the only worthy husband was the Moon itself, and when it was full, Moon was duly approached by the proud parents.

'I am almost too honoured by your approach to speak,' came the reply. 'But what is honour without honesty? There is a suitor far worthier than I, for does Sun not outshine me?'

Mr and Mrs Mouse were secretly relieved that they had not married their daughter off to an inferior contender and could hardly wait for morning to arrive.

'I am almost too overwhelmed by your suggestion to utter,' came Sun's response. 'But what is compliance without candour? Cloud is far mightier than I as he covers my brightness with ease.'

Outraged that Sun had wasted their time by shining so brightly, their prayers for the day to cloud over could not be answered soon enough.

'Your scheme puts me on a pedestal,' stammered Cloud. 'But what is gallantry without generosity? Wind is far more powerful than I as he blows me effortlessly around the heavens.'

Rattled by this narrow escape, Mr and Mrs Mouse wished on Cloud the wind that he deserved and did not have long to wait.

'Your proposal all but silences me,' whispered Wind. 'But what is acceptance without acknowledgement? Although I blow Cloud around the sky, Hill stops me in my tracks.'

Most put out that Wind had wasted their time, the doting pair climbed Hill.

'Your plan all but makes me crumble with joy,' rumbled Hill. 'But what is delight without duty? I must tell you that Bull gouges great grooves in my slopes each day.'

Furious at wasting their efforts on an inferior, the mice found Bull in his stall.

'This idea is most flattering,' bellowed Bull. 'But what is felicity without fairness? Each night Rope ties me to my stall. How can I marry when I am so easily bound by another?'

Indignant at the trouble they had taken over such a weakling, the fond parents approached Rope.

'Your scheme makes me grow quite limp with desire,' lisped Rope. 'But what is love without loyalty? You would soon discover that each night my very fabric is nibbled away by Master Mouse.'

Contemptuous of such a lacklustre lover, Mr and Mrs Mouse scuttled off to find Master Mouse, who instantly accepted the hand of their daughter. He and she lived happily ever after.

Snake in the Grass

The Golden Age of Camelot had passed. The glorious deeds of chivalry and the adventures full of mysteries would be remembered for centuries, but Arthur's court at Camelot was no more, and the country was plunged into strife. The Knights of the Round Table had disbanded, torn apart by divided loyalty to Arthur or their objections to the liaison between his wife and his strongest and dearest knight, Sir Lancelot.

No knight was more pleased at this disarray than Arthur's own son, Mordred. Not only had he waited years for this to happen, but he had used every opportunity to sow dissent, spread scandal and drive a wedge between his fellows wherever lack of trust or argument provided an opening for him to do so. But who could have blamed him for holding a grudge against his father – the king who professed such moral values and expected so much from others, but who had tried to have his own son murdered as a baby?

Mordred had been conceived, just as Arthur had been, by the use of sorcery. Knowing that Guinevere would never conceive a child and provide Britain with an heir, Arthur's half-sister, a powerful sorceress, had used her enchantments to lie with Arthur and conceive his child. Arthur was horrified to hear that he now had a bastard son conceived through incest and he could think only of how he could prevent this shameful secret from getting out. Knowing that the child would be in danger from his own father, his mother had hidden him by leaving him with a foster family to raise. However, not being able to find his son for that reason, Arthur secretly ordered a search for all the boy babies of the right age. They were then seized from their families and sent out to sea on a raft so that they would drown.

All of them perished, except for one, and that was his own son Mordred. Arthur knew that he had the blood of many innocent babies on his hands, but he did not know that his own son had survived and that ordering the murder of all those innocents had been a truly purposeless crime.

Mordred had been washed up on shore unharmed, where he had been found by a fisherman. Being childless, he and his wife had been glad to raise him as their own. However, they had been watched from afar by Mordred's birth mother, who was content to leave the child in their care for his own safety. When she judged the time was right, she came to him and told the young man about the true circumstances of his birth.

Mordred made his way to Camelot and revealed to the whole court who he was. Arthur's chalice, once so brimming sweet, was now running over with poison. But he did not know how far that poison would spread – he did not know whether this young man was also aware of how his father had tried to have him killed and instead had been the death of many innocent children. He knew that Mordred could blackmail him with this secret if he knew the full truth, but there was no way of finding out how much Mordred did know, without implicating himself. It was possible that Mordred would hold this knowledge like a secret weapon and strike with it whenever he wished.

Fearful of what he might be able to do, and wanting to appease or even win him round, Arthur acknowledged his son. He accepted him with open arms, and knighted him. A malign and poisonous creature had been welcomed into the once perfect garden of Camelot.

This new knight infiltrated every corner of the court, watched everybody without being seen to do so, found weaknesses, bided his time. If there were those who had chosen to turn a blind eye to Lancelot's more than courtly love for Guinevere, there were those who could easily be persuaded otherwise. It didn't take much to spread the poison through rumour, through accusation, through confrontation and challenge.

The knights dispersed, Lancelot returned to Brittany, Arthur followed to help him with his battles there and Britain was left vulnerable. Mordred summoned those to whom he had been whispering poisoned words over the years, and from these he created his own army with which to seize the crown. To shame his father further, he added insult to injury by trying to force his own stepmother to marry him. Guinevere, who in happier circumstances should have been his actual mother, managed to gain sanctuary in the Tower of London whilst civil war raged. Arthur and Lancelot returned from Brittany too late to save a ravaged land, but in time to negotiate for peace by offering a truce.

The documents were drawn up and ready to be signed publicly by Arthur and Mordred. With so little trust, the opposing armies were also present, Mordred's far larger than Arthur's. The armies stood at a distance whilst a chosen few of the nobles drew close to witness the signing. They were unarmed, having made a show of leaving their weapons on the ground before approaching the canopy under which the treaty lay waiting.

Mordred was to sign first, but just as he leaned forward to place the nib of his quill, a noble standing behind Arthur saw a movement in the long grass. It was an adder, snaking its way towards the king, moments away from his unprotected ankle. Instinctively he seized his knife to plunge it into the snake and protect his king. The rapid gesture was immediately noticed by the other side, but worst of all, they saw the glint of sunlight on metal.

'Treachery! Treachery!' they cried out.

It had seemed to them, unable at that distance to see the snake in the grass, that one from Arthur's party was bent on stabbing Mordred as he leaned forward. His army charged towards the other, all thoughts of peace forgotten.

The two armies re-engaged, and amidst the slaughter, man against man, son and father were searching for each other with murder in their hearts. Very few of Arthur's knights had survived when at last he came upon Mordred. Arthur seized a spear and ran him through with it. So great was the son's loathing for his father, that, unable to free himself from the spear, he drove it deeper into himself so that he could drag himself up its shaft towards the man he hated. Handhold by handhold he dragged himself towards Arthur until he was able to deliver his father a mortal blow before dying himself.

So ended the last battle. So it was that a snake in the grass put an end to the dream that was Camelot. By the River Cam on Cadbury Hill you can walk over this place where only the grass remains, whispering this sorry tale.

God's Bargain with the Worms

'… I'm going in the garden to eat worms,
Big ones, small ones, wriggly ones and juicy ones,
I'm going in the garden to eat worms …'

Long ago, God allocated various foodstuffs to all the animals, thus creating a balanced diet on a global scale. As usual whenever gifts were given, not all were satisfied. The worms arrived last on the scene having had to worm their way through so many layers of earth to wriggle into the Divine Presence. Convinced that not enough would be left for them, they were already complaining about the lack of choice. Ever eager to please, God allocated the fat of man and woman of all the races of the earth as their food.

'But it will have to be dead first.'

Nevertheless, they had certainly been given a plentiful and varied diet compared to many other creatures and were, for a while, content. Sadly for the human race, when they learned of this, they were appalled to think of being eaten by worms when they were buried. Some even got round it by inventing cremation. An example of this is that of my own father who was named Ernest. He insisted on being cremated as he 'Did not want worms making love in dead Earnest'.

Most, however, began to fret and worry. When it came to their burials, they were worn away with anxiety, their bodies mere husks of skin, with no fat on them. Now the worms definitely had cause to complain, and the fact that it was a very long way to wriggle up to Heaven, did not improve their tempers.

Had St Peter been invented at the time, they would not even have waited for those pearly gates to open. As it was there were far too many clouds to crawl over before they were before the Celestial throne.

'Leave it to me. I'll think of something,' said God with a sigh.

We all know what it's like when you grab at a solution under pressure – we don't always think of the long-term consequences. God invented money. People were so busy thinking about how to make, spend, get, borrow, steal, and invest money that they forgot all their worries about what would happen to them when they died. When they died it was once more with a layer of fat. Some who were particularly good at spending money died fatter than others. The worms were happy. Nothing delights them more than the obesity epidemic sweeping the Western world, and no matter how much they eat, they never get fat themselves, just longer.

On the Wing

The Fly and the Flea

A flea and a fly in a flue were imprisoned
'Let us flee,' said the fly
'Let us fly,' said the flea.
So they flew through a flaw in the flue!

Bat Woman

The moated castle where this tale took place can still be visited. You can still see the alcove where an ancient retainer lived off the passage that led to what are now the estate offices. She was so old and had been there for so long that nobody quite knew where she had come from. If anybody ever paused to wonder at it, rumour told that she had once been nurse to several generations of the lord's children.

The busy servants hurried past, barely noticing the dark bundled shape covered in a huge black shawl. For years beyond counting few ever connected her temporary absences to the appearance of the full moon. Who would notice at dead of night along that dark corridor, that the alcove was empty? What people did notice was that during those full moon nights, above the lake that fed the moat, there always fluttered a solitary bat. Moreover, it was there every month of the year, not seeming to hibernate like others of its kind.

In time a young lord inherited, and wanted to curry favour with the monarch. One of the ways of doing this was to 'discover' witchcraft, and deal with the perpetrator by the severest of punishments, which was that of being burned at the stake. The harmless and supposedly helpless old woman would be a suitable target for the new lord's excessive zeal, so he had her watched. That is how the pattern of her absences during the full moon and the appearance of the bat was established. As it was believed that witches fly when the moon is full, it didn't take much stretching of a wicked and accusing imagination to suspect her of using magical powers to transform herself into that night-loving creature.

She was dragged out of her hidey-hole and sent to the lock-up to await 'trial'. There she waited for a public burning in a cell that didn't even have a window. Gaolers were instructed to watch her around the clock. A few nights later fire broke out at the castle and much of it was destroyed. This took the young lord's mind off the prisoner, who summoned the gaoler on duty. She told him to bring her a stick of charcoal and the man replied that he had been instructed to only let her have her ration of bread and water. Perhaps he never suspected that such an old woman could move so quickly. Her skinny fingers shot between the bars and pulled out some hairs from his beard. Everyone knew that if a witch had something from your living body such as hair or nail clippings, she could cast spells on you. His mind moved swiftly from shock to fear when she spoke.

'If you don't bring me a piece of charcoal, you apology of a man, I will turn you into the weasel that is your true nature. I will make sure that neither family nor friend will recognise you and all will vie to be the first to set their dogs on you. So bring me a stick of charcoal do, while you can still walk on two legs.'

He scuttled back with it so quickly that he nearly put his candle out. Fearing to get close, he thrust it at her through the bars. One hooked hand grabbed it, and then she blew upon her other, open hand. There were three tiny crackles followed by the acrid smell of burning hair. He had done what he had been told and there was no need to carry out the threat. With a sigh of relief he withdrew; what harm, after all, could an old woman with a stick of charcoal do?

He remembered this same feeling of relief from another occasion, when he had been lucky enough not to have been on duty when a prisoner had escaped. Over time that prisoner had chipped away at the old mortar with his pewter plate, singing loudly to cover the sound of his efforts. He had replaced the mortar with strips of rags torn from his own clothing whenever the gaoler was due. As his clothes were a similar colour and had been folded to represent the texture of the mortar, nobody had noticed anything. Since that embarrassing episode the order had been given to whitewash all the walls on the inside.

When she was alone, she took up her own candle and stared intently at the whitewashed surface of one of the walls. She had already felt that it was colder than the others, so she knew that her freedom lay on the other side of it. Muttering to herself, she used the charcoal to draw a window. It had bars befitting a prison cell, but no horn or glass between them. Then, widdershins, she began to spin. As she spun, her black shawl swirled around her, unfurling like wings. Still spinning, she shrank to the size of a man's hand. Then, squeaking, she flew upwards towards the bars in the window. Still squeaking, she negotiated their spacing exactly, flew through them and away.

Far below, by the light of the full moon, she could see what remained of the still smouldering castle. How good it felt to fly over her beloved lake once more. Inside, the young lord was poking about amongst the wreckage. Above him nobody had noticed that what they thought was merely a charred beam was in fact burning slowly through the middle from the inside. Its charcoal centre had become too soft to hold that heavy oak timber together. It disintegrated in the middle, and the ends came away from their fire-loosened joists. One of the heavy pieces landed on the man below, pinning him to the ground. By the time he was found it was too late to save him. Some said that was a blessing given that his face, lying in those smouldering embers, had been horribly burned away.

When the moon had set, the old woman returned to her home. The passage with her alcove had not been harmed. All was more or less the same as she had left it, apart from some items that the servants had rescued from the fire and placed there. Now she had a comfortable chair to bundle herself up in, and even a footstool. When a servant came to retrieve these pieces, she showed no surprise to find the old woman ensconced.

'Well there you are, Granny. We was wondering when you would be back, and here you are all wrapped up snug as a bug in a rug where you belong, and entitled not to be disturbed at your age. But I might just send our Annie along to see you, she's grown a fearful crop of warts since you've been gone.'

The furniture was reported to be too fire damaged to be of any further use.

War or Peace?

Hark! Hark! his matin praise
In warblings sweet the lark doth raise
To Paradise above …

Now the brook doth pause to hear
Whilst hiding 'neath the rushy ground
So heav'nly tender is the sound
That comes mankind to cheer.

Some say that it was between the King of Ulster and the King of Leinster that the argument began. Some say that it wasn't the King of Leinster at all but the King of Munster. Whichever it was, kings should have known better. Grown men should have known better, shouldn't have let it get out of hand in the first place. There they were at a feast when one of them boasted that his court piper was the best in the land. Well, in those days, your piper was your pride, your joy and your reputation. The other king was not going to let that remark pass.

It is easy to boast when you are thick with drink, and harder to back down. The boasts turned to argument, the argument to insults, the insults to jeers, the jeers to threats. The courtiers looked on aghast and none had the skill to turn the hostility aside lest it was directed at themselves. There were no weapons in the feasting hall, but there were plenty outside. No one knew how things had escalated so quickly before the two kings were shouting challenges to war, and were just about to shout orders to their armies, when their hoarse voices were drowned out by another sound.

The piper who had been the focus for this jealousy was making the loudest possible sound on his bagpipes. It was terrible. Nothing else could be heard. Everyone covered their ears. Goblets rattled on the tables, hounds howled under them. Very gradually, he reduced the volume. The drunken kings swayed in the blessed silence. Then, very quietly, the piper spoke: 'Two kings will go to war over the skill of their court musicians. Whoever wins or loses will only prove the skill of their armies, and their willingness to waste innocent lives. Yet if these pipers were set to play, turn and turn about, all would rejoice in the music and a judgement could be made as to which is the better. Let music be her own judge, not the railings of drunken men.'

Only a piper could have got away with speaking to a king like that. The horrendous cacophony had cleared their heads enough for them to hear the wisdom in his words. They agreed to the suggestion. Everyone sighed with relief. The other piper was sent for and the competition was arranged for the next evening. They were to play turn and turn about from moonrise to dawn.

How shared skill and love of one's art brings out the best in oneself and one's competitors. Those pipers played as they never had before, each delighting as much in what they heard as in what they played. The hours passed. Not a note was lost nor a tune repeated. The inky night was seeping towards grey and the people grew uneasy – the musicians were equally matched – no mortal could judge between them and war still threatened.

The sky lightened and the musicians, exhausted, fell silent. Dawn's golden touch streaked across the land. A lark rose from his nest and shot up towards the pearl-pale sky. As he rose, he sang. The tiny bird's song soared beyond his flight – opened dew-clenched daisies, drowsy eyes, dulled minds. With one gesture the pipers pointed upwards, and rose to greet their better self. All strained to see that point of heavenly music in the brightening sky. When at last he plummeted down to silence, his fellow musicians clapped and called out that surely Brother Lark was the best of the pipers in all of Ireland. The contest had been won and war was averted.

That same day, those pipers composed a tune in which they recorded the lark's song. It is a double jig entitled, unsurprisingly, 'The Lark in the Morning'. You can hear the skylark singing all the way through, and it is as popular amongst traditional musicians today as it was when first composed.

The Children of Lir

Long ago in Ireland, kings were chosen from amongst the chiefs, not born to inherit the crown. When the new king was elected, Lir was displeased when he was not chosen and refused to take an oath of loyalty to the new king. He, in turn, feared what might happen with such a powerful neighbour who opposed his leadership. Moreover, the other chiefs were angry with Lir for not accepting the vote of the majority. Disunity was a dangerous thing.

Soon after, Lir's wife died. Their marriage had been childless, which was a great sadness to him. Now that Lir was a widower, the king saw an opportunity to make an alliance. He suggested that Lir might like to marry one of his daughters. At last Lir would have another chance to become a father and he was pleased that the king's daughter accepted him. At that point, he swore an oath of loyalty to the king, who was also about to become his father-in-law.

Both men were delighted when the first child was born. The girl was named Fionnuala, which means white shoulder. It was a name praising her beauty in a culture where fair skin was highly prized. Her parents could not have realised how prophetic that name would prove to be. A brother followed and then twin boys. Their mother did not recover from their birth and died soon after. So it was that Lir had become a widower for the second time.

The children's grandfather did not want them to grow up motherless and suggested that another of his daughters should marry Lir. Aoife had always loved her niece and nephews and was glad to become their stepmother as well as their aunt. All lived happily together and the children thrived. Perhaps Aoife also wanted children of her own, but that did not happen. Neither could she have said when it was that her love for her stepchildren turned to jealousy. As she watched her husband playing with them, doting on them, that jealousy turned to hatred. Her hatred flourished like a poisonous fungus spreading unseen beneath the ground where everyone treads. But it was also flourishing inside Aoife until it seemed to have wrapped itself around her every thought, her every breath. She knew she would have to get rid of those children if she were ever to breathe freely again.

She had her chariot harnessed and told the four that they were going out for a ride. Her servants followed, and when they were in some remote place she spoke secretly to them, saying that the children had stolen Lir's love for her. She had hoped that this would make them pity her and make it easier for them to accept bribes of gold to murder the children. When they refused, she decided to kill them herself, but did not have the courage to follow it through. Instead she told them that they would all go swimming in the lake as a treat to end their outing. When the children were splashing in the water Aoife cast a spell that turned them into swans.

As they watched their slow but inexorable metamorphosis, Fionnuala, whose pale shoulders were now covered with the white gleam of feathers, called out that they had friends who would not desert them even in animal form. She begged for the spell to last for a specified time rather than forever, and Aoife granted that the enchantment would be off them in nine hundred years. As she watched the children she had once loved becoming beasts, she relented enough to grant that they retain the power of human speech – an act that would seal her own doom.

When father and grandfather discovered that the children were missing, the servants directed them to the lake. There they joined the crowd who had already gathered to hear the swan children's story. Still gifted with human speech, they sang of their betrayal and their voices raised in song were the sweetest thing that had ever been heard in the whole of Ireland. The king turned to his daughter and asked Aoife what was the worst creature she could imagine. She replied that it would have to be a spirit of the air, buffeted by the winds and knowing no rest or home.

'So be it then, so be it by your deed and speech,' said her father.

He took from beneath his robe a magic wand and struck her with it. Aoife rose wailing into the air and was swept away. When wild winds rage over that lake, people still say that they can hear Aoife weeping and raving at her fate.

For hundreds of years the Children of Lir, in their swan forms, lived over lakes and sea. Blown off course and separated by storms, they nevertheless found each other again due to the efforts of Fionnuala, who bore the fate of the siblings upon her shoulders. Wherever they encountered people, they filled hearts with joy with their singing. Because of their stepmother's curse, their sorrow was greater than anyone's. So it was that all who listened to them were healed from their own troubles. People travelled from all over Ireland, from across the sea and even the Otherworld to hear the Children of Lir.

In those times it was forbidden to kill any swan in any part of the island. During one particularly severe winter, their great webbed feet were frozen into the surface of a lake. They raised their voices to Heaven, to the new God that St Patrick had brought to Ireland, and pleaded for the welfare of all their bird brethren. Their prayer was heard and they no longer suffered from the elements. All this time, the people knew where they were because of their singing, including those holy brothers who were the carriers of the new religion.

Unfamiliar as most were with the new ways of worship, the younger swan children were frightened at the sound of a bell calling the faithful to prayer. It was Fionnuala who told them not to be afraid and that such a bell would be the source of their salvation. When the voice of the bell fell silent, the children raised theirs and were heard by the holy brother. He welcomed them and placed silver chains around their necks, tokens of their royal origins and above all that they were under his protection.

They had not sought sanctuary for long before word spread that the Children of Lir had come to live on land. The Queen of Connaught wanted to claim them, so her husband sent a messenger ordering them to be transported to their court. This their protector refused. Unused to being disobeyed, the angry king came to fetch them himself. Still the monk refused to allow him to break the law of sanctuary. The king seized Fionnuala, but as soon as he touched her, feathers came away in his hand. The shrine was filled with a whirling cloud of white feathers, settling like drifting snow as the enchantment fell away from the children. But they were children no longer.

Before monk and king stood an ancient woman and three ancient men. Their skin was withered and lined like bark, their limbs twisted as ancient hawthorns. Fionnuala held out her knotted hands to the monk and begged that they be baptised as their death was upon them. As soon as this was done, they died and their bodies crumbled to dust. The monk buried this in the same grave.

So ends the story of the Children of Lir, one of the three great sorrows of the land of Ireland, and some say, the greatest of the three.

The Swan Captive

Far out on the fens was a deserted place where people feared to go. Not only did people avoid it, so did all the wild birds except for the swans. Sometimes there were so many of them that you couldn't see the water at all, the swans had turned it white so it looked like the ice was melting in early spring. In the centre of the swans was a group of seven, all larger than the others. They were always together like they had come from the same clutch, but hadn't dispersed after a year like other swans. At the sound of their great wings beating the air, people would fall silent with fear. If they happened to look up and catch sight of them, they knew it was bad luck unless they went home and refused to open the door to anyone.

In the nearest village lived a fowler who was such a good shot that he was nicknamed 'Robin Hood' – maybe that's why he had more courage than most. When a great hunger came to those parts, he decided to shoot a swan. In those days, just like today, all swans belonged to the Crown, but then it was a hanging offence to take one. It was such a deserted place he knew that he could get away with it, and none of the locals would tell. He thought he might as well take one of the largest of the birds and, knowing that the seven swans would be flying over just before sunset, he waited for them in his boat. As they passed, he managed to shoot one of them in the wing and drag her into the boat. She was powerfully strong, beating at him with her sound wing, hissing and pecking at his eyes. What he didn't expect was that the other six would go for him too. He managed to hold them off with his iron knife until the boat thankfully drifted ashore.

He dragged the swan into the hut where he kept his tackle, but when he had lit the lamp and saw the wounded creature bleeding, he changed his mind about killing it. Instead he took up some strips of sail cloth to bind up the wound. As he was doing this, he noticed that the wing was becoming an arm, so pale he had never seen skin like it before. The swan was changing into a woman, the loveliest ever seen. The fowler took her as his wife and kept her captive.

The six swans who had attacked him flew round the hut all night, crying and beating against it. At first he gloated over his prize, but as the six returned night after night, he grew afraid. It wouldn't be long before news of this strange behaviour would leak out, and who knows who would come to find out more? He hid his fear from the woman. Her wound was healing well. On the seventh day, it was quite mended. When he looked at her arm, it began to sprout feathers and he was terrified. As he backed away from her, she became a swan once more. She lunged at him hissing furiously and there was no avoiding her blows. He was scared witless at her power, so he ran outside his hut.

There the other six were waiting for him. They drove him into the water, where they pinned him down until he drowned. Then their sister joined them and the seven swans flew around in a great circle seven times and flew away, never to be seen again. Even though the swans had gone, no wild birds every went to that place ever again.

Robin's Red Breast

'Who killed Cock Robin?'
'I,' said the sparrow,
'with my bow and arrow,
I killed Cock Robin.'

Tradition tells us that Robin acquired his red breast during the crucifixion, when he tried to relieve Christ's agony by removing thorns from his crown. Some say that he is still stained with Jesus' blood to remind everyone of his kindness. Others say that he was stained with his own blood as he impaled himself to help Jesus, and has borne the mark of this sacrifice ever since. Apart from being our most colourful and tame winter bird, Robin is also associated with Jesus' birth and is the most common image on Christmas cards.

Gotham's Cuckoo

The cuckoo is a witty bird,
She cometh with the spring.
When autumn winds are blowing,
She spreadeth wide her wing.
The winter she disdaineth,
She shuns the rain and snow,
With her I would be singing
Cuckoo! Cuckoo! Cuckoo!
And off with her I'd go.

Reports of the first cuckoo song of the year are still featured in the media. Many of us like to hear an early cuckoo as their unmistakeable sound means that, even with our variable weather, spring cannot turn back on itself. The foolish inhabitants of the village of Gotham are no exception, and every autumn they hold their unique 'Chasing the Cuckoo' festival.

This event recalls the time when an item appeared on the parish council meeting agenda, exhorting villagers to be suitably prepared for the wintry months ahead. Possibly because they recalled how their plans for a better winter had once been betrayed by an eel (see page 94), they decided that it would be much easier to dispense with the colder months altogether. Noticing that these appeared when the cuckoo disappeared, they decided to prevent the cuckoos from leaving.

As the summer days shortened, every man, woman and child was put on the cuckoo watching rota. Signs of avian restlessness were noted – ruffled feathers, extra preening and wing flapping were documented. As each cuckoo soared in flight, it was followed by its allocated posse of pursuers. Since they needed to run whilst watching the sky, their cross-country progress was not an easy one. Nevertheless, they stumbled and tumbled, splashed and crashed their way across stony ground, through quagmires and woods in relentless pursuit. Because it was all worth it. Sadly all the cuckoos escaped, taking summer with them. It seemed that the would-be jailers had escaped too, as none of them returned. This is because they were too stupid to ever find their way home, but are still looking, which is why fools can be found all over the world.

Those remaining Gothamites celebrate these heroes every autumn when the winners of each class in the pondweed weaving contest run off in all directions to commemorate that mighty chase. Needless to say, the population of the world's fools is added to at every summer's end.

However, this homage to tradition did not solve the problem of the cuckoos' departure. The following year it was decided to be prepared well before the cuckoos arrived. A dense hedge was planted that would have been the envy of any RSPB education officer. Growing in the shape of a perfect square, it flourished with so thick a foliage that a wren could barely perch on an outermost twig. When this prison was completed, it was time to bait the trap. A shrub was placed in the empty space in the middle. Its branches were laden with nests created by the Gotham Village Twig Knitting Society. Every child donated their Easter eggs to tempt the wily cuckoo, and they did not need to wait for long.

Mrs Cuckoo laid her own eggs in each nest and Mr Cuckoo sang for the prescribed four months. Then, in the middle of August, great was the Gothamites' dismay when they took to the skies and disappeared. An emergency parish council meeting was called. It was agreed that the plan's failure was only temporary as the hedge merely needed more time to grow. A motion was unanimously accepted for the villagers to put their own motions to the task of aiding its growth. To this day they faithfully stick to the night soil rota. The by now rectangular hedge is a well-known silhouette on the horizon, warning travellers of their proximity to England's village of fools.

How the Birds Got Their Colours

When birds were first created, they had been given no colours. Maybe their fluttering and swooping, waddling and splashing, let alone their calling and singing, had been enough to delight their Creator at the time. So it was that they were all black or white or a combination of these. Giving them colours was an afterthought, but nevertheless accomplished with great thoroughness.

An announcement was made that any bird who wanted to receive colours was to appear the next day before the Creator's throne. There they could choose whatever colour combination they wanted. What could be more generous than that? Even before dawn could reveal the rows of colours that had been placed in front of God's collapsible travelling throne, there was the Creator with brushes at the ready. So too was the queue of birds that stretched beyond the horizon.

At first light, the work began, but began with an unfortunate incident. The Magpies, ever pushy, had managed to get to the front of the queue. Nevertheless, they were arguing amongst themselves as to which particular magpie should be first. The Creator tired of their squabbling and squawking and ordered them to go away until they could behave. They were unable to stop arguing and so never received their colours. That is why they are still black and white. That is also why Magpies are still scolding and quarrelling to this day, each one blaming the other for starting it.

After that the work continued apace, with every bird receiving the colours they asked for, and which you can still see in all their glory. Some needed a little help: Chickens, for instance were rather lackadaisical.

'Oh anything, anything will do, just get on with it we're very busy, places to scratch, dust to scrape,' they cackled.

So the Creator had great fun flicking them with splashes of tawny and russet as they scratched and bobbed. Pigeons were too shy to decide.

'Yooooou chooooose, yoooou chooooose,' they cooed.

Sensitive to their modesty, God applied touches of subtle mauve and green that shimmered only when caught by the light. Swan thought that she was already perfect, but was persuaded as a favour to Divinity to have a brightly coloured beak. And so it went on until there was another hitch. That rare visitor, Oriole, had appeared and asked for gold. Maybe it was because Oriole is so hard to see, high up in the canopy, that gold was requested – but there was none.

'I don't have any gold,' said God. 'I have always thought of gold as a metal not a colour.'

'Well I am most disappointed in a Creator who can't provide gold pigment, especially when one has been invited to ask for whatever suits.'

'Now just a minute,' said God, possibly remembering that unfortunate affair with Hedgehog. 'I didn't say you *couldn't* have gold, just that *I didn't have any ready!*'

Before them appeared just one tiny pot of gold paint, and Oriole, thereafter known as Golden Oriole, was satisfied. Species followed species and it seemed a miracle that all got their colours by the time the light had almost gone. Even the owls had acquired theirs in the twilight, and were too wise to mention that the paintbrushes had spattered rather in the gloom. Pleased with a good day's work, the Creator was just about to fold up the throne and go home, when a faint coughing sound was heard beneath it. A little dusty grey bird emerged, hardly visible in the growing dusk.

'Ahem, ahem, don't forget me, I want my colours please.'

'What time do you call this? You're too late, it's night-time now.'

'Well all the other birds have got their colours and now it's my turn.'

'Yes, but they were there when they should have been. Anyway, there aren't any colours left, they have all dried up.'

'That's not fair. It's not my fault that I have to work at night and sleep in the day. That's how I was made. All the other birds have their colours and I want mine.'

The little voice began to quaver and the beak to tremble. Of course, God was moved to pity.

The pots were re-examined. There was a tiny gleam at the bottom of the smallest pot that could only be seen because the moon had just risen from behind the trees. Because it had been made last, the pot of gold hadn't completely dried out. There was a single moist bead at the bottom. The little grey bird was ordered to stand completely still and open his beak. The finest brush was seized, the bead of gold paint clung to its point and it was flicked towards him. There was a tiny flash of gold in the moonlight, before it landed at the back of his throat. And that is why from that night to this night, Nightingale sings with a golden voice.

How Magpie Taught Nestbuilding

One for sorrow,
Two for joy,
Three for a girl,
Four for a boy,
Five for silver,
Six for gold,
Seven for a secret never to be told.

There is much folklore about Magpies, generally thought to be an unchancy bird with thieving ways. Early in the year they can often be seen in groups sizing each other up before competing for nesting sites, and this habit may have given rise to this children's chant.

Long ago it was Magpie who taught the other birds how to build nests. She started with Kingfisher, showing how to enlarge holes in the sandy riverbanks and digging them into tunnels. She showed Owl how to use the hollows in tree trunks and Oystercatcher how to shape beach pebbles into a bowl shape. Mud was rolled and shaped for Whitethroat and Swallow and twigs woven for Robin and Thrush. Tit was shown how to line her nest with soft moss and Coot was taught the merits of high-rise architecture when surrounded by water. The Pigeons were the clumsiest of all, their piles of untidy twigs shaming their teacher. Cuckoo was quite unteachable and at that point Magpie gave up.

Very much later, when all the other birds had been given their colours, with the exception of Magpie, her attitude changed. Jealous of her feathered companions' newfound beauty, she decided to collect rent in arears. That is why, from that day to this day, Magpie robs every nest she can, eggs and chicks alike.

What Swallow Tells her Chicks

I slept in an old homestead by the sea:
And in their chimney nest,
At night the swallows told home-lore to me,
As to a friendly guest.

Quaint legends of the fireside and the shore,
And sounds of festal cheer,
And tones of those whose tasks of love are o'er,
Were breathed into mine ear.

Horatio Nelson Powers

When we see the swallows returning, we know that summer cannot turn back on itself. We think of these migrating birds as visitors from Africa. Does this mean that in Africa people think of swallows as being British, particularly as they or their descendants were born here? This story too has migrated with the swallows from the Middle East, but as the mother swallows chatter it to their British-born children, it has found a way into this book.

Long ago there had been trouble in Paradise. The Garden of Eden was finally settling down after Adam and Eve had been expelled. Snake was happy to follow them because he knew that wherever humans were to be found, it was easy to make trouble.

The animals of the Earth were curious about Adam and Eve – after all, no humans had been seen outside the gates of Paradise until then. As the pair rested disconsolately on the dry ground, so different from the lush greens of the Garden, all the animals crept up around them. Soon they had to smile at the squeaking, roaring, fluttering, jostling crowd as each tried to get a look or a sniff of these strange beings. Amongst them of course was Snake, and this crowd would prove to be a not-to-be-missed opportunity – for making trouble, of course. Although trouble for trouble's sake was always worth the effort, there was also something to be gained here. Since leaving Paradise, Snake was uncertain as to what or who he should be eating in this new world. Now was his chance to find out.

'My dear friendsss,' he hissed.

All the animals fell silent. Instinctively they feared Snake. They watched and listened warily.

'We have all journeyed far and must all be hungry. This has caused me to wonder which of all the creatures amongst us has the sweetest flesh. It would of course be quite improper of me, as the poser of the question, to express any opinion on the matter. May I suggest that one amongst you takes on the responsibility of settling this important issue? To give you plenty of time I recommend that we allow a year and a day to allow sufficient opportunity for sampling. Now who is going to volunteer?'

Well, Adam certainly wasn't. He already knew which was the sweetest flesh, that was precisely why he was there in the first place. There was an uneasy stirring amongst the animals, who sensed this could get dangerous. However, without a second thought, Mosquito piped up – he did have a brain half the size of a gnat's after all.

'Oh please let me do it!' he whined. 'I've always wanted to travel. When my wings get tired I can always hitch a ride. I'm so light my hosts won't even notice.'

Nobody else wanted the job, so it was left to Mosquito. He had a wonderful time travelling around the world, sampling the taste of all those who gave him a lift and tasting many more who didn't.

Meanwhile, Adam and Eve had built themselves a house and created a small vegetable garden. Eve would water it lovingly as it had been planted with the seeds that she had been allowed to take from Eden (and how that happened is another story). The water made muddy mounds around the plants and Swallow found that these were perfect for nest building. Little curved plastered walls, formed from tiny balls of mud, were stuck beneath the eaves of the new house, around the door and chimney. As Eve's belly grew, Swallow laid her eggs. When these hatched, she worked even harder to feed her chicks and so kept Eve's garden free from insect pests.

The months were running into seasons. It seemed no time at all before a year had passed. One day later, all reassembled to hear Mosquito's verdict.

'I have travelled the whole wide world and sampled the blood of every creature that lives on land or flies through the air. It is my certain opinion that the sweetest flesh of all is the flesh of...'

But Mosquito didn't get any further, because Swallow knew what was coming next. She had seen the red welts and lumps that had appeared after every night on her human friends' bodies. She had seen how they scratched and writhed with the discomfort caused by Mosquito's many relatives. Just as Mosquito uttered the first sound of the word 'Man', Swallow flew at Mosquito and plucked out his tongue. So it was that what Mosquito actually said was: 'It is my certain opinion that the sweetest flesh of all is the flesh of Mmmmm!'

'Pardon?' said Snake. 'Speak up can't you!'

'Friend Mosquito has a sore throat,' said Swallow. (That much was certainly true.) 'He has asked me to speak for him. He was trying to say that the sweetest flesh of all the creatures belongs to Frog.'

Quick as a whip, Snake turned on Frog and swallowed him whole. Frog tasted disgusting and Snake knew he had been tricked. Furious, he lunged at Swallow. Eve was anticipating more trouble from Snake and, at great risk to herself, just managed to stand on his tail in time as Swallow launched herself into the air. If it weren't for Eve's quick thinking, Snake would have swallowed Swallow whole too! But he did manage to snap at her tail, and take a bite out of it.

That is why, from that day to this day, Swallow's tail has a piece missing from the middle and retains such a distinctive shape. That is why snakes eat frogs and mosquitoes can only hum 'Mmmmm'. That is why, from that day to this day, people are always happy when swallows nest on their houses, because some of them remember how they saved each other from Snake's wicked ways.

This is the story that Swallow is telling her chicks, when you can hear them all twittering by your windows and chimneys.

The Rooks in the Pear Trees

There was once a carter whose route took him past a hedge in which were growing some magnificent pear trees. It was spring and they were so covered in foaming white blossom, that it looked like five fountains had mysteriously appeared amongst the hawthorns. The humming of the bees was so loud that he couldn't hear his horse's hooves. He passed that way again at the end of summer and the boughs were hanging low with fruit. This time he couldn't hear the hooves for the buzzing of the wasps and hornets that were feasting on the overripe fruit. Careful to avoid them, the carter chose a plump pear – then another, and yet another. He had never tasted anything so delicious, and wondered at them having been planted in a hedge in the middle of nowhere.

Just then a farmer rode by and the carter hailed him and asked about the trees. Although he seemed none too pleased at this enquiry, he directed him to a public house that lay slightly out of his way.

'I'm not the one to tell that story, but the landlord knows all about it, he was there. Ask him.'

It is a short road to a good drink and a shorter one to a good story. In no time the carter was at The Sign of the Pear Trees. He explained that a farmer had sent him to hear the story from the landlord's own lips. When he had heard a description of the farmer, that landlord allowed those lips a luxurious smirk before he began: 'That same farmer owned the best pear trees in the whole county if not the whole country. But you know what pears are like, a tricksy fruit, hard as marbles one minute and soon as you take your eyes off them, soft as whey the next. Trouble was that close to those trees there was a great rookery, and those rooks were also watching the pears. Try as he might, the farmer could never get to the ready-to-pick fruit before those rooks. Every year he would come over to tell me about what happened and drown his sorrows with a few extra pints. He would tell how those birds descended like a silent black cloud. What enraged him as much as their thievery was that for this one occasion in the year, they had the cunning to remain silent, the better to prolong their subterfuge. Course, even if he managed to scare them off mid-feast, the fruit would be damaged beyond saving.

'One year, I made a suggestion and he took me up on it. He chose a day that he guessed was just before the pears' ripening. He got a ladder and painted every twig and branch with sticky bird lime. The next day was extra warm and the pears had ripened by noon. The expected black cloud descended, but finding themselves stuck fast, the rooks were not silent for long. The farmer rushed off to get his blunderbuss to take advantage of those sitting targets. When he appeared with it, those birds started flapping their wings harder than they ever had. But it wasn't in a kind of frenzied panic, it was more like they had been drilled on a parade ground. Flap, flap, flap, all in time. With that concerted effort, didn't they all lift up into the air, tearing those pear trees out by the roots and bearing them aloft.

'Farmer was too flabbergasted to take aim, his blunderbuss only went off by accident when he sat down hard with his knees giving way at the shock. The birds were out of range by the time he could reload. Anyways, I was in here when I heard something tearing at my thatch. Couldn't make out what it might be, so I rushed out to see, just in time to see that great flock passing over. It was the roots of the pear trees dragging across my roof that I had heard. Well, I admit that my knees nearly gave way at the surprise too, when there was a mighty clap of thunder and a downpour. Didn't that rain wash off all the bird lime! The rooks flew free, dropping those trees in my hedge – I own a few fields here and about – where they took root from that day to this. Course I turn a blind eye if Farmer ever comes scrumping, and now you know why he prefers not to tell this tale himself.'

The Honey Bees and the Snow-White Hare

In a time when our bee populations are under threat, there is a growing awareness of what bees do for us. Apart from these busy pollinators being essential for the future of our crops, they play an irreplaceable role in the maintenance of worldwide flora. As well as providing food, their honey is used to heal wounds and their pollen to treat allergies. We burn their wax as sweet-scented candles and use it for polish. It is recognised that this remarkable animal has special sensory powers and colonies have been trained to detect cancers in humans before our most sophisticated medical equipment can do so. There is a revived interest in the folklore of bee keeping and the tradition of telling the bees important family news is still practised.

A young man kept a smallholding in the folding foothills of the mountains. Although he tended his vegetables and livestock well, his main love was for his colony of bees. In the spring, they would fly out over the moor and their honey would taste of the golden gorse flowers that bloomed from February to December, for as the local people said, 'Gorse will bloom until kissing goes out of fashion.'

As the days turned warmer, the bees would forage on other flowers, but it was in the late summer that their pollen harvest was at its most bountiful. In August, with the blooming of the heather, they would fly far over the purpling swathes of moor. Geordie's heather honey was famous all over the county and though he took pots of it to sell at the market, he sold just as much to people who were happy to walk all the way to him for some. Kindness itself, he would often slip a piece of honeycomb to a poor child or make up a small pot for rubbing onto an old man's aching joints.

People wondered whether Geordie wasn't lonely living in such a remote place all by himself, but if they asked him he just laughed and said he had his bees for company. Certainly, many passing that way had heard him talking to his hives. They had heard the warm sound of buzzing swell in response to whatever he was murmuring to them, just like the distant waves of conversation you could hear between friends.

'Do you understand them or do they understand you?' they would ask.

'A bit of both, a bit of both, I should think.' And that easy laugh would come again.

But how did he manage for company in the winter when his friendly bees were asleep? That remained a mystery.

One day, just as summer was leaning into autumn, he heard the sounds of a hunt coming towards him over the moor. He shuddered with dislike for a sport that depended on the suffering of living creatures. Looking up apprehensively from the hives he was tending, he saw a streak of white against the heather whose purple was now tinged with brown. From time to time his eye lost sight of it as the animal zigzagged amongst the clumps of heather. Then, as it drew closer, he could see that it was a hare. She was making for his cottage and was now so near that Geordie could see that her strength had gone. The pack was closing on her, so he opened the gate, fearing that she might not clear it. With no time to lose, she had leaped into his arms and the pack was baying all about him. He stuffed the hare under his jacket and drove the hounds out of the garden with a rake.

'Have you seen a hare?' cried the laird, who was also master of the hunt. 'You couldn't miss her, all white she is from nose to tail.'

'What I have seen is the damage your hounds have caused to my vegetable patch!' said Geordie, trembling nearly as much with his newfound courage as was the hare beneath his clothes.

Taking the hare into the safety of home and hearth, he marvelled at her pure white coat. He had only seen white hares on the slopes of the mountains in winter. Then their coats turn from brindled brown to white, blending with the snow, protecting them from eagles. Then he noticed her eyes. They were as blue as a summer sky, and that he had never seen in a hare before. He had seen those with brown eyes so dark that they echoed the peat pools on the moor, he had seen those with eyes as golden as his honey, but never blue.

First he gave her water, then he tended the sore pads of her paws with honey. He fed her on hay with honey dribbled over it. That night she crouched in an empty log basket by his bed. The next day he carried her to the hives and told the bees that another companion had come to live with them. Then the hare was free to hop and nibble all around his small plot of land, always within leaping distance should danger threaten. Soon it did. The bees began buzzing in a way that he seldom heard, a particular quality of sound that they made only when feeling menaced. A stranger was coming, and the hare leaped towards him for reassurance. He picked her up and cradled her in his jacket and then he too began to feel on edge. At first he thought she might have come for some honey, but instead of the polite greetings one would expect, she stared at his hands. Perhaps it was his dead mother's gold wedding ring that she coveted, but then she said, 'I'll buy that hare from you.'

It was hard to hear those words, the bees were roaring so loudly. His tongue was a stone in his mouth. 'She is not for sale.'

'I'll give you a gold piece for that hare.'

His words were heavy, slurred as one soaked in mead: 'I'll not sell her, I tell you.'

His heart raced at the same pace as the hare's, pulsing in his hands, but his legs were the trunks of bog oak beneath the peat pools on the moor. Her hands reached toward the hare and his feet were rooted deep with the twisted gorse bushes. Anger sawed the air behind him, a furious buzzing as a single bee landed on her hand and stung. The air swelled with buzzing as bees from hive and moor formed a black curtain between woman and hare, driving her back. After that the hare had bees to guard her wherever she went. But what would happen when the cold weather came and they went to sleep for many months?

Geordie was worrying about this when he heard the clip clopping of hooves. By came the gypsy's wagon – a shout, a hand raised both in greeting and farewell. They were going further south for the winter.

'First frost came on the slopes last night, Geordie, we'll be seeing you next spring!'

It was some time after they had gone when he saw the shape on the road. Running to look, he saw that it was a sack of grain, feed for the gypsy's horse that had fallen from beneath their wagon. It would be dark soon, and a long way back for them by the time they missed it. Geordie set his own pony to the cart to follow with their sack of grain. Dusk was greeting night and the bees were asleep. He did not want to leave the hare alone so he took her with him, riding inside his jacket.

At last he caught up with the wagon. Gypsy Joe had already set up camp and had been apprehensive at the sound of an approaching cart. Farmers didn't like gypsies as a rule, so he was relieved to see who it was and so thankful when he learned why Geordie had come. He found it hard to believe how kind he had been in going to all the trouble with a long trip home. But all Geordie would say was that he couldn't bear to think of a hard-working horse going hungry. Just as he turned to go, Joe noticed the creature peering from his jacket into the lamplight, and asked what it was.

'That's no hare. I should know. No hare ever had blue eyes. It might look like a hare, but if that's a hare I'm gentry.'

Not having land to farm, gypsies often lived on what they could find on the moors and in the woods. Some called it poaching, but they called it surviving. Many a bonny brown hare had been cooked in Joe's pot, so who would know if not Gypsy Joe? There was someone else who would, right there in the wagon. Joe's old mother had heard everything, and she spoke up.

'Geordie you bring that creature to me now!' You didn't disobey old Mother Boswell, and when you obeyed you did so quickly.

The old woman held the hare. For all she was blind, she had the second sight. Her hands felt the warm shape like a mother nuzzling a newborn. Her fingers searched inside the snowy fur like seedlings pushing through dense earth. But it wasn't light they were looking for, it was truth.

'Blue eyes you say? Well that explains it. This is no hare; I can feel the body of a woman in here. She's been bewitched into a hare's shape. You'd best be telling me what's been happening.'

So Geordie told her everything, and he didn't forget to say how concerned he was that with winter coming, she would lose the protection of the bees.

'Yes, that's worst of it and that witch will be coming into her full power before long at All Hallows' Eve. That's when she'll try for her again and the worst of it is that this year the moon will be full, which will make her strength wax all the stronger. She'll not risk approaching you again, she'll be working her magic from afar.'

Then Mother Boswell told Geordie what he would have to do. He went home and told the bees about his visit to the gypsies. He asked them for their help. Even though they were sleepy with the growing cold, he knew that they had heard him because he could hear a humming in the hives that grew to a buzzing that swelled to a roar.

The next night was Halloween. Geordie took a length of twine. He knew the struggle would be fierce so he melted some beeswax and coated the twine with it to make it less harsh on the hare's coat. He tied one end around her neck and the other around his left wrist. Then he set his pony to the cart and opened all the doors and windows before climbing up into it, the hare beneath his jacket as usual. As the last of the October sunlight dipped behind the moor, he was off as quick as the pony could trot. On they went through the darkness, as far and as fast as they could.

Then Geordie felt the hare buck against his ribs. He knew then that it must be midnight. Stopping the cart, he held her with both hands. It was as well she was tied to him, otherwise, strong as he was, he would never have been able to hold her for long, compelled as she was to come at the witch's bidding. He had played thrashing salmon and unbroken horses with greater ease, but still he held on, trying to get that faithful length of twine to bite into his wrist rather than her neck. The moon was passed her zenith and began to set. The movements became less violent, but the creature became heavier in his arms. Stillness came. In his arms was a woman. He cut the twine that threatened to choke her. She took his knife and cut the twine around his wrist. But they were bound closer than before. She could not remember where she came from, but was glad to be here. She could not remember who her people were. Geordie and the bees were her people now.

Redstart Brings Fire

Long, long ago it was not an everyday occurrence for people to see birds. These lived mostly in Tir na n'Og, the Otherworld, the Land of Eternal Youth. The gods used them as messengers, sending them to our world from time to time as omens of joy and hope.

Those who had died passed over to the Otherworld, to Tir na n'Og, and could choose eternal youth in exchange for losing all their memories. There were some, however, who did not choose to forget everything about their former lives. These remained the age they had been when they died and went into the halls beneath Tir na n'Og where fires had been lit for them. There they told stories of past times and no matter how often the tales of the heroes of old were told, they were always new for those who listened. Sometimes the gods themselves came and sat with the departed around the fires, telling stories from before our world began and stories of what was yet to come. When Angus Og, god of love and youth, joined them, the birds that flew around his head sang until their hearts were young again.

One of these was Redstart, a small dark bird barely noticeable amongst all the others with their colourful plumage. How she too loved to hear those stories. How she relished the comfort of the fire when she returned from Earth, where she had been singing the gods' message of joy. She noticed that the old people especially liked to draw close to its warmth and thought how those on Earth would also like to be able to enjoy having fires. Redstart asked the gods if she could take fire to them and their leader finally said, 'You may take fire with you to Earth as long as you only give it to one who is unselfish, kind and good.'

A brand of perpetual fire was placed in her tail and Redstart departed with her precious burden. When she arrived, she felt overwhelmed by her task – Earth was so big and she was so small, how could she find the right person with whom to entrust fire to? The first man she approached didn't know what fire was and tried to kill her. It was obviously going to be much harder than she had imagined, so, trembling with fear after the attack, she went to Owl to ask for help. Owl advised her to tell her story to Plover, Lark and Seagull so that they could tell all those on Earth and Sea that Redstart had a priceless gift for the one who was the kindliest and least selfish.

Her helpers flew far and wide with this news and before long many men had converged on the bush where she was perched. Each one of them boasted about how good he was, but each, on hearing the other's accounts, grew angry and jealous of his fellows. Soon fights were breaking out, and Redstart, fearful of the violence, flew away. By now she was so weak that she couldn't go far and fluttered down to the ground outside a cottage, where she lay helpless.

A little girl came out, picked up the exhausted bird and brought it inside to show her mother. The woman was nursing her youngest and told the girl what to do to make the bird comfortable, promising to feed it by and by. Redstart was grateful for this kindness. She wished that she might be given the fire, but how could her deeds compare with those great and heroic ones that she had heard around the fires of Tir na n'Og? Nevertheless, she asked her if she was good and unselfish. The woman laughed.

'Good and unselfish, me? I wish I had the time to be good and unselfish! I haven't a spare moment between caring for my husband, our children, the new baby and another on the way. Just to feed us all, in the spring I must dig, sow and plant. Summer passes with weeding and tending the beasts out on the pasture and autumn is taken up with the harvest. If the seasons have been kind there is even more to reap and prepare so that I can give it to my neighbours who are old and cannot work the land as they used to. In the winter there is the curing and spinning and weaving so that we may all be clothed and shod.'

All this was said as she comforted a toddler who had fallen over, stirred the pot for the family supper, and placed a shell of sweet water before the bird. Then she went off on some other errands. Redstart asked her rescuer to bring her some twigs and some pine cones. The little girl brought these and the bird asked her to fashion them into the shape of a nest. This being done, she crept into it and used her tail to set it alight. When the woman had finished taking her neighbour some milk, pulling some healing herbs that she had planted for an ailing sheep, putting the toddler to bed and singing the baby to sleep, she found fire burning on her hearth.

The gods rewarded the little bird by giving her fire-coloured feathers to remind everyone of that heroic journey. From that day to this, the Redstart is also known by country people as the 'Firetail'.

Reclaiming the Right to Roam

Braving the Boar

Foranan O'Fergus, the physician, would travel the land of Ireland tending to the sick. Wherever he went, people would gather to see him treating the patient and to pay their respects to the good man. Whenever he was called upon he would rise and arm himself, not against his fellow men, for nobody would attack such a famous and revered physician, but to defend himself against savage beasts. In those not so distant days, before the island's forests had been chopped down by invaders, boar, wolf, wild cat and lynx would not hesitate to attack a lone traveller. However, his truest weapon of all was Flann, his great wolfhound, who would fearlessly defend him against any danger.

One day he received a call to a far-off place that lay over a mountain. As it was urgent, he decided to shorten the journey by climbing over, rather than walking around it. He took with him his climbing pole, made of holly wood. This had been handed down from father to son, through the generations, just as their medical skills and knowledge had been. So old was this stick that he couldn't guess which grandsire had first owned it. Age-blackened and as hard as iron, its point had never blunted nor its shaft snapped in the rockiest ground.

Foranan was to regret his choice of route for the rest of his long life. Having climbed the mountain with faithful Flann always at his heels, his way led past a lake that held a legend in its depth. It was said that this water – whose name meant 'The Lake of the Hound' – had the power to send up a champion fighter – man or beast – to match any who challenged it. It was also said that no mortal creature had ever beaten that fiendish champion. Nevertheless, pride or recklessness still claimed its victims from time to time. There were those unbested by any man who could not believe that they could be conquered by anyone from this or the Other World. Summoning a champion of whatever kind they chose, they not only met their match but their demise. Even prize stallions and bulls had become sacrificed at the altar of their owners' ambition.

The doctor was a man of science, not superstition. He can't have believed in the tale and was moreover a gentle man whose life was devoted to the relief of pain and suffering, much of which was brought about by fighting. Maybe it was the power of that lonely place, maybe it was the wicked spirit beneath the waters grown hungry from neglect that influenced Foranan to call out across the waters: 'There is none valiant enough to vanquish my fell hound Flann!'

The calm waters seethed, gathered themselves into a huge wave that towered above man and dog, then retreated, tearing up the gravel and shingle from bed and shore before roaring towards them with all the sounds of Hell. Stones were flung about all around them, but those that did not fall took on the shape of a monstrous dog that attacked Flann. They fought for hours until the close of day, when the fiend dragged the dog's broken body beneath the lake's surface and he was never seen again. All that long night the doctor mourned the loss of his friend and cursed his own foolishness. He would never be able to forgive himself for the rest of his days. Moreover, his rashness had delayed his journey to a patient, and so he hurried on through the darkness, across broken ground, trying to make up for lost time.

He blundered on until dawn. Incautious through distress and lack of sleep, he gave the farrowing sow plenty of time to hear and smell him before he noticed her. The wild sow was edgy with the hunger brought on by having ten piglets to feed. Now she smelled meat. Rage stiffened legs and bristles as this intruder advanced, threatening her newborn litter. She charged. The rattle of loose scree brought him to his senses.

'If only Flann were with me now, my life could be saved!'

The physician was so steeped in loss that this was his one thought as the vicious pig bore down upon him. He knew that he was far less of a match for this furious, ravenous creature than Flann had been for the monstrous lake hound, but maybe he was inspired by his companion's courage. Somehow, he wielded his climbing pole so that as she rushed at him, its point passed into her mouth and down her throat. Her strength and speed forced its point through her hide and, piercing outwards, it reappeared beneath her ear. As wild boar will, she fought her way up the pole to slay the one who had turned from prey to killer.

Borne down by her bulk, Foranan felt her power ebb away as he lay beneath her. Still holding the holly staff that had so far saved his life, he managed to crawl free. As he pulled it from her wound, the blood gushed down over the rocks and in the growing light the man could see that below him lay another lake. Despite her great weight, using his climbing pole as a lever, he managed to roll her body over the cliff into the water below. He completed his journey, attended to his patient and told the gathering of his adventures. From that day to this, the lake has been called Lough na Muicka, which means 'The Lake of the Pig'.

Boars' Break for Freedom

Discussions about reintroducing wild boar had been ongoing for years. Some were concerned about dangers to walkers and dogs, and others were eager to reintroduce a native species that could revitalise forest habitats. During this debate, wild boar were making a comeback, but only in captivity. Boar farms were being created for those whose sophisticated palates craved a tangy flavour and a texture that fought back when chewed. It wasn't long before the whole boar fought back against captivity before being turned into sausages. Like some of our favourite national heroes, they tunnelled beneath the barbed wire and made their Great Escape to freedom.

They were prepared to sample domesticity again, but only on their own terms. These involved visiting domestic varieties of sows who lived on farms in the region. It may be that their captors had sought to keep any Great Escapes a secret; however, evidence of these soon became obvious when litters of piglets were born sporting stripy pyjamas and stroppy dispositions.

Rewilding the boar took on a new meaning when animal rights activists released one hundred of them from their prisoner of war camp. They charged through the East Devon village, where my stepdaughter was given an eyewitness account by her friend who tried to outrun them with a toddler in a buggy. Realising that she would soon be overtaken by the porcine tide, she escaped by throwing the buggy over a garden hedge and following it. No animals or humans were hurt in that escapade.

However, this form of rewilding, unsanctioned by any authorities, could not go unchallenged. Hunting with dogs had recently been made illegal, but the Exmoor Hunt, perhaps with a flash of foresight tempering their traditional vision, was still fully functional. Rumour has it that with many a 'Tally Ho' and 'Tantivvy' the hounds were let slip in the field to round up the escapees, hopefully along with a few activists as well. Thank goodness the Exmoor Hunt was on the case, as they triumphantly brought to earth one boar out of the hundred.

Since then, quiet visitors to Exmoor will be blessed with the sight of peacefully rootling wild boar, doing their bit to improve the soil for all our surviving native species.

The Grateful Wolf

Perhaps Foranan O'Fergus' reputation as a healer had spread to the animal kingdom as well as amongst Ireland's parishioners. As he was returning from a visit to a patient, he paused to drink at a stream just before dusk. When he had finished, he turned to see that a large she-wolf was staring at him. Naturally, he froze with fear, but thus restrained from any precipitate action, he was able to notice the unusual. With her were her litter of young cubs. If she were hunting, she would not have brought them with her. Neither would a she-wolf be hunting alone. Furthermore, the wolf was sitting upright like a huge dog, not crouched on all fours as though about to spring.

The animal must have sensed a subtle change in the man, because she changed from an alert to a submissive posture, lying on her belly and stretching her forepaws in front of her. It was then that he could see that one of her paws was swollen and oozing. Had she come to him seeking help as so many of God's creatures had done? Foranan had never treated a wolf before, but decided to proceed as he had on occasion with large dogs who might be unpredictable because of their pain. However, he did not risk trying to bind her muzzle, but tempted her towards the cooling water by splashing it gently towards her.

It was as though she understood him completely. First she gathered each cub in turn by the scruff and laid them amongst his gear, making the noise that meant in wolf language, 'Don't you dare move until I come and get you.'

Then she joined him by the stream. When he had washed her paw, he could feel that there was something that had penetrated between the claws and entered the pad. Removing it would cause even more pain. She looked at him with unwinking yellow eyes. It was as though he understood her completely, her look said, 'I am Wolf, I endure hardship.'

Deftly, he removed a sliver of wood. The wolf did not flinch. Blood and puss flowed from the wound. Now came the most dangerous part of the procedure. To make sure that the infected gash healed, Foranan needed to apply ointment and a bandage, which were in the pack where the cubs were nestled. Would she attack if he approached her young? Slowly, gently, he lifted one and handed it to her. The huge jaws opened and tenderly she placed the little bundle beside her. Foranan breathed easier with the others. He took out was what needed, applied a healing salve and a bandage. The wolf rose, called her cubs, and limped off towards the trees. She turned once and grinned at him before disappearing amongst them.

Three days later, early in the morning, Foranan was awoken by a commotion outside. Trampling and breaking sounds were coming from his garden, and then the unmistakeable sound of mooing. He had no cows, being often away and unable to look after them, but now there were three cows in what remained of his vegetable plot. From their condition it was clear that they had travelled a long distance and had not had a comfortable journey of it. On the ground was the bandage that he had wrapped around the wolf's paw.

The physician was relieved that the cows had been driven from outside the area – he did not want any neighbour accusing him of theft. But how to return cattle that had been stolen by a wolf? How to find their owner? Word spread throughout the region, but none came to claim back the wolf's payment of the physician's fee. Many said that the story of how Foranan O'Fergus had the skill to cure a wolf was compensation enough.

The Return of the Wolf?

Passionate arguments for and against reintroducing the wolf have been heard for some time. Farmers are sure that their flocks and herds will become its prey. 'Rewilders' believe that wolves only come into conflict with livestock when their habitat is destroyed – and that there is plenty of wilderness in Scotland to avoid this.

Certainly in this part of the world, the wolf is an animal of menace in most people's imagination. Perhaps this is because it is so similar to ourselves – sociable, cunning, highly organised and a top predator.

The Sea Eagles' Revenge

The physician Foranan O'Fergus couldn't have known that he was about to tend his most curious and tragic case when he set off with the party of women who had called for him. They were strangely silent on the way, which was most unusual, and Foranan could tell that they were in a state of shock.

At last they reached a part of the coastline that boasted high cliffs. There the inhabitants had a particular fondness for horse racing and would let their horses graze unattended on the rich sward that grew on the clifftops in the summer months. When Foranan saw his unconscious patient, he predicted that the man would only have three more days of life. He could tell immediately that he had fallen from a great height, but his injuries were not consistent with most victims of cliff falls. Every bone in his body had been broken, but his very length had been compressed like a concertina. Never having seen injuries like these before, he asked if anyone knew what had happened.

Gradually his subdued companions began to speak and told him what they had witnessed. The dying man had been mad for the racing and had always kept his own horses. Small and slight of build, he had always kept his jockey's figure and was a redoubtable horseman. Recently he had bred a filly that was the light of his heart, so sure was he that she would win every race. As ever she was left to roam and graze on the clifftop with the others. It was summer and the people were working hard all day at their patches of land or out to sea. No harm had ever come to the horses who were left to their own devices until the autumn.

Lately, the sea eagles had grown bolder and more cunning, but nobody thought that they would attack anything as large as a horse. However, a child had reported seeing them trying to harry some of the beasts towards the cliff and drive them over the edge. The eagles would wait until the sun was at the right height over the sea to dazzle the horses, then they would swoop at them from behind, to make them bolt towards and over the cliff edge. Perhaps the child was not believed, or people were too busy to react. Soon after, the girl was up with the dawn to gather the mushrooms that flourished where the horses had manured the ground. In the low slanting light of morning, the birds were at last successful and drove the highly-strung filly to her death. Seeing this happen, the child went and told the owner, who went near mad with grief when he found her corpse at the foot of the cliff.

Swearing vengeance on the eagles, he returned with a knife to that spot. Many of the villagers followed him, some wanting to see what he would do and some hoping that they would not have to restrain him from some act of folly, so enraged was he. He tried to shoo his neighbours away, knowing that the eagles would not come near if they saw people. However, nobody wanted to leave and instead they hid themselves in a brake of ancient holly trees to see what would happen next.

They watched the horseman skin the corpse. They watched him open up the carcass and empty all the contents from the body. Some of these he rolled underneath it and some he smeared onto the flayed hide. Then he climbed into the body cavity and covered himself with the filly's skin, with the smeared entrails uppermost, and waited.

Wonder mixed with horror as the witnesses told the physician what happened next – what they could still barely believe. Unsuspecting, a mated pair of eagles arrived and landed on the carcass. Perhaps the grieving owner had not been expecting two birds at once. With a great shout he lunged from his hiding place and grabbed each bird by the leg, so that he held one in each hand. But with both hands full, he couldn't wield his knife. For a moment it seemed that his revenge would exceed his expectations, but if so, that was his undoing. Maybe if he had let one of his prey go, his knife hand would have satisfied his anger. If he had let one of them go, what happened next would not have been possible.

There was a tremendous thrashing of wings and those mighty birds rose into the air with their assailant borne aloft between them. Nobody would know if it was rage or surprise that prevented him from letting go. Soon it was fear and not revenge that made him grip all the tighter as he was carried even higher towards the top of the cliff. No strength of grip could save him then as each bird, with their free set of talons raked at his clenched fists until he loosened his grip and went into freefall.

The poor man's injuries and the appalled expressions of the witnesses, who concurred with every detail, left the doctor in no doubt that this was a true account. A cliff fall would leave marks that showed the way in which the victim had rolled and bounced. The jockey's skin was unblemished and his height had been shortened by a foot at the impact of his landing. Foranan, the best bone-setter in Ireland, could do nothing for him. When he passed away after three days, the doctor wrote an account of this, his strangest case, which can be seen to this day.

The Return of the White-Tailed Sea Eagle

This spectacular bird, with the widest wing span of any eagle in the world, was almost extinct in these islands. Apart from some very rare sightings in the Hebrides and Shetlands, they had disappeared from the rest of Britain and Ireland due to the Victorian mania for taxidermy and egg collecting, as well as hunting and poisoning. Their demise was also brought about most successfully through the long-term unforeseen effects of pesticides.

Had they survived they might have mitigated the devastating effects that the accidental introduction of mink has had on our native wildlife. The white-tailed sea eagle is the only animal that catches swimming mink, which is otherwise as elusive as it is predatory. In North America it is this eagle that keeps this voracious threat to birds and small mammals in check.

Where it has been reintroduced in certain parts of Scotland, farmers complain that they lose up to 20 per cent of their lambs. There have also been reports of sheep weighing 60kg being killed. These accounts lend plausibility to the previous story about the death of the jockey. Described as being particularly small, he could easily have weighed less than a grown sheep. The pair of mature birds would have been using all their combined strength to escape their assailant, and it is quite believable that they would have been able to carry him to some height.

Now that these magnificent eagles have returned to Scotland and Ireland, there are plans to reintroduce them to the South of England, to the cliffs of the Isle of Wight. This most southerly region of the United Kingdom is not known for its rugged terrain, but rather for its neat farms, picture postcard villages and orderly holiday resorts. How fitting that this regal bird may fly high above one of Queen Victoria's favourite residences. Its giant shadow may glide across the seafronts made so popular during her reign – one that sought so hard to tame Nature, pinning her to boards and displaying her locked up in glass cabinets.

Lynx the Most Beautiful

Lynx knew that she was the most beautiful creature in all of the forest. On still days, she would shimmy along a branch that overhung the lake, in order to admire her reflection. The black tip of her tail would twitch with delight and the tufts on her ears would perk up with pride. Even her whiskers would stand to attention at the loveliness of her image.

One day, she was most put out to see her mirror being disturbed. Worse still, there was Otter laughing up at her from the water with his row of pointy teeth.

'You think you are soooo beautiful, Lnyx, with your tufty tail and your tufty ears and your dark spots. I bet you don't know how many spots you have, though, do you?'

Before she could ask what Otter was willing to bet, he had disappeared. This was just as well because she had no idea how many spots she had, and the thought rankled. It was probably Otter who rankled most of all. She hated to admit that there was a creature who was as agile as herself, and she had never managed to catch Otter. What a delicious fish-flavoured saturated fatty snack he would make. She hated to think that Otter could get the better of her, and determined to find out how many spots she had.

Lynx started to count her spots but got in a muddle as she could never remember where she had started. She had also never learned to count but was not going to admit this to herself. Reluctantly she padded off into the forest to ask for help, and unsurprisingly the other animals were reluctant to give it.

She managed to paralyse Rabbit in the headlight gaze of her yellow eyes and promised not to harm him if he helped. With trembling paw Rabbit started to count, although he hadn't learned how either.

'You have exactly as many spots as there are dandelions in the grass!' he squeaked and scampered off.

Lynx decided she wanted a second opinion. She caught Field Mouse in the cage of her claws and promised her freedom if she helped. Whiskers aquiver Field Mouse started to count, but she hadn't learned how either.

'You have exactly as many spots as there are berries on the bushes!' she squeaked and scuttled away.

This was beginning to sound good. A third opinion could do no harm. This time a loftier one would provide more of a range. Owl was not best pleased at being awoken. He had the sense not to mention that he could barely see in the daylight and did not refer to the fact that he had never learned to count.

'You have exactly as many spots as there are stars in the sky!' he hooted and retreated into his trunk.

Lynx was so elated that she lost her usual sense of caution. As she slunk down the trunk, she saw a movement in the leaf litter and pounced. Just in time she realised her mistake and cat-jumped away from Adder.

'In a hurry, Lynx?' he hissed.

Lynx knew, like all the other animals, that Adder was the cleverest because he was a snake. He was also rather beautiful, but she managed to ignore that.

'Just trying to find out how many spots I have, friend Adder.'

'Well, you've had three answers, how many more do you want?'

For an animal that was completely deaf, he nevertheless managed to overhear everything, which just went to show how very clever he was. Lynx thought it time to go back to Otter with her answer.

She shimmied along her favourite branch and admired her reflection as she waited. She was good at waiting and it was particularly easy on that branch with such a lovely view. All too soon, Otter broke her mirror again.

'Well, there you are beauuuutiful Lynx. And do you know how many spots you have?'

'I have exactly as many spots as there are dandelions in the grass, berries on the bushes, and stars in the sky!'

'I wish there were as many fish in my lake!' said Otter and Lynx was left to her mirror once more.

The Return of the Lynx?

*The lynx, once a native of our forests, is at the top of the rewilding list. It
has been extinct in Britain since the late medieval period.*

*An area in Yorkshire that was then thickly wooded seemed to abound
with lynx, normally rather solitary creatures. This could have been due
to the destruction of their habitat elsewhere. Licences were granted to hunt
them, as they had become a threat to livestock. Perhaps it was due to an
abnormally high population and competition for dwindling food sources that
the following attack occurred. The account was attributed to the fifteenth
century, but some say it must have happened in the fourteenth.*

A knight on horseback was attacked by a lynx as he rode home
alone. At first it attacked his mount, and although wounded,
his horse managed to escape. Then the lynx turned its ferocity
upon the rider. Assuming that he was not wearing armour (his
journey was mundane and not associated with fighting), the
man had only his sword to protect himself. The battle between
man and beast was prolonged and wide ranging as it terminated
in the porch of the local church, where each creature died from
the wounds it had received from its adversary.

The horse, returning without its rider, covered in lacerations,
obviously caused alarm in the household. A search party set out
and eventually found the bodies of knight and lynx where they
had died.

This seems to be the only account of anyone having been
attacked by a lynx in Britain or Ireland. Shy and retiring
creatures, they are unlikely to attack livestock if wild food is
available to them. They are being considered as a solution
to deer culling in Northumberland's Kielder Forest and the
Scottish Highlands, as they would keep deer populations under

control. Since deer's natural predators have been wiped out, they can become a threat to the health of forests by overgrazing, eating saplings and killing mature trees by stripping their bark. Culling is a controversial practice and reintroducing this beautiful predator may replace it.

The Crane Skin Bag

Aoife and Iuchra, two beautiful women, fell in love with the same man. Iuchra now saw her friend as a rival and planned vengeance. She invited Aoife to go swimming with her and whilst she was in the water, that most magical and transforming of elements, she turned her into a crane.

When asked how long she would remain in the form of this bird, Iuchra replied that it would be for two hundred years, and that she would be banished to the court of Manannan, the god of the sea, who dwelt beneath the waves. There she would stay and be mocked for being a flightless crane who could never fly over water or onto land. Moreover, when she had lived out those two hundred years, her skin would be taken and turned into a bag.

All this came to pass, but Manannan, to honour her, kept his most precious treasures in the crane skin bag. In keeping with his marine nature, it was said that when the tide was rising the treasures could clearly be seen. When the tide was on the ebb, the bag appeared to be empty. The treasures included objects of great magical powers, some made by the ancient gods themselves, and which over the ages were passed from hero to hero. Today, storytellers refer to the crane skin bag as the magical repository for the great treasures of lore and wisdom that are carried in traditional stories.

An Eyeful of Crane

In 1812, a relic was entrusted to the Ulster King of Arms who was compiling a pedigree of the O'Donnels of Donegal, Ireland. Although at first thought to contain a relic of St Columcille himself, it proved to contain a document probably written in the saint's own hand, and containing a story of rivalry that some call today the 'first instance of contravening copyright', which a pet crane sought to prevent. Curiously the word pedigree comes from an observation of the crane's anatomy, and is derived from the French 'pied de grue' *which means 'crane's foot'. It was noticed that its structure resembles branches as they are drawn on a family tree – hence our word 'pedigree' which is a corruption of the French pronunciation.*

In Ireland cranes were often kept as pets, possibly because of their ability to imprint easily with humans. There are also instances of their being kept as guard animals, their extraordinarily loud voices and vocal dispositions being perfect for raising an alarm. This story seems to combine both these characteristics.

In a time when religious manuscripts were all handwritten and extremely valuable, St Columcille was visiting a colleague, St Finnian, from whom he borrowed a book. Unbeknownst to his host, St Columcille would secretly copy out this manuscript when his duties of the day had been finished. He did this in his darkened church, miraculously lighting his work with light that spilled from the fingers of his right hand as though they were candles.

On the last night of his visit, just before the copy was finished, Finnian sent a messenger to retrieve the book. Being afraid at the strange light coming from the church, the messenger put his eye to a crack in the door. St Columcille sensed that he was being watched. He told his pet crane that if God permitted it, the bird had his permission to pluck out the spy's eye. The crane then thrust his beak through the crack and plucked out the messenger's eye. Somehow the messenger managed to retrieve it and took it back to St Finnian along with the story of what St Columcille had been doing. Finnian blessed the eye and replaced it, and it worked as well as it had done before.

However, he was furious about the copy that had been made of his book without his permission. A judgement about the ownership rights of this copy was eventually made by the High King of Ireland. Displeasure at his decision eventually led to a great battle, after which Columcille exiled himself from Ireland and went to found the great religious settlement on Iona, where he became known as St Columba.

The Return of the Crane

Cranes have recently been successfully reintroduced to England. There are now colonies breeding in the wild in Somerset and Norfolk. Indeed, one Somerset bird spurned an arranged marriage and found her lifelong partner all by herself in Norfolk. Curiously, whilst these birds were still in captivity as part of their carefully managed induction programme, wild cranes also began to appear. The author was not the only enthusiast to see a flock of these before their captive cousins were released.

Extinct in Britain and Ireland since the mid-1500s, they must nevertheless have been a major feature in certain wild landscapes and were also characters in domestic life. Research shows that they were the third commonest pet in Ireland and there are records of fines being levied for harming what was considered to be a domestic creature – and still is in other parts of the world. Archaeological evidence provides glimpses of how this extraordinary bird was revered in pagan times and in the Early Celtic Christian era.

In a time when habitat loss is accelerating the demise of so much of our native wildlife, the reintroduction of the crane is a triumph of the 'rewilding movement' and a symbol of hope for our future.

An Unkindness of Ravens and a Parliament of Owls

Owls and ravens are two of Britain and Ireland's most iconic birds, so much so that they almost merit a chapter of their own. Perhaps our oldest stories of these come from that incomparable Welsh collection, the 'Mabinogion'.

One story tells how Bran, whose name means 'Raven', was King of the Land of the Mighty, which we now know as Britain. He went to the defence of his sister Branwen, 'White Raven', to rescue her from an ill-fated marriage. The battle that ensued left few survivors, and Bran's loyal companions carried his still-speaking head long after Bran's death. At last they laid it to rest under a mound that would become the base of the Tower of London. There it lay, facing towards the Channel, to repulse invaders.

This legend is remembered in the enduring presence of the Tower's raven community. To this day, you can visit the ravens, kept in the luxury provided by their Ravenmaster. It is said that if there are no ravens living in the tower, Britain will fall into enemy hands. Nevertheless, some have gone to live elsewhere, as did the raven who was rehoused in London Zoo after attacking Her Majesty's Rolls Royce, causing thousands of pounds worth of damage. No doubt it was seen as a rival due to being so very black and shiny. The author knows of a wealthy gentleman who is the owner of a pet raven. He would warn his dinner guests against arriving in evening dress because too many dinner jackets and black silk dresses, despite their décolleté, had been shredded.

Until recent times, owls have been seen as a bird of ill omen. In the 'Mabinogion', an unfaithful wife conspires with her lover to kill her husband and is punished by being turned into an owl. She is told that this is a fate worse than death because, in her new form, she would never be able to show her face in daytime, as a reminder of how she had shamed her husband. To appear as an owl during daylight hours would ensure that she be mobbed by other birds. The author thought this was allegorical and not a natural phenomenon, until witnessing it herself: an owl had been surprised in daylight and was surrounded by many other species, who had corralled it against a tree trunk and kept up a cacophony of alarm calls until night fell. All that time, the owl did not dare attempt an escape until rescued by the dark.

Other tales of punishing owl transformations abound: Suibhne (Sweeney) High King of Ireland, was transformed into an owl by St Ronan and compelled to live alone in the wilderness. This was not just for rejecting Christianity, but for actively thwarting the saint's mission by acts such as throwing his bible into the sea, only to have it returned by an otter. Jesus was said to have turned a baker's daughter into an owl for her meanness at giving short measure of the loaf she had baked from the dough entrusted to her. It is this story that Shakespeare refers to in Ophelia's line, 'They say the owl was a baker's daughter ...'

Nowadays, due to the influence of modern literature and feathered friends such as Wol in 'Winnie the Pooh' and Hedwig in 'Harry Potter', we tend to associate the owl with wisdom:

> A wise old owl lived in an oak
> The more he saw the less he spoke,
> The less he spoke, the more he heard,
> Why can't we be like this wise old bird?

Bibliography

Berry, James, *Tales of the West of Ireland*, Colin Smythe, 1842

Briggs, Katherine, M., *A Dictionary of British Folk Tales*, Routledge & Kegan Paul, 1971

Jacksties, Sharon, *Somerset Folk Tales*, The History Press, 2012

Jones, Gwyn and Jones, Thomas, *The Mabinogion*, Everyman, 1993

Joynt, M., *The Cathach of St Columba*, The Irish Church Quarterly, Vol.10 No.39, July 1917

Lang, Andrew, *The Grey Fairy Book*, Dover Publications Inc. NY, 1967

Leodhas, Sorche Nic, *Thistle and Thyme*, Bodley Head, 1962

Muir, Tom, *The Mermaid Bride*, The Orcadian Ltd, 1998

O'Sullivan, Sean, (ed.) *Folk Tales of Ireland*, University of Chicago Press, 1966

O'Tuathail, Lorcan, *Crane Notions*, Careful Publications, 2016

Swire, Otta. E., *Inner Hebrides and Their legends*, Collins, 1964

Thompson, David, *The People of the Sea*, Canongate Classics, 2001

Tongue, Ruth, *Forgotten Folk Tales of the English Counties*, Routledge & Kegan Paul, 1970

Wilson, Barbara Ker, *Scottish Folk Tales and Legends*, Oxford University Press, 1975

Society *for*
Storytelling

Since 1993, The Society for Storytelling has championed the ancient art of oral storytelling and its long and honourable history – not just as entertainment, but also in education, health, and inspiring and changing lives. Storytellers, enthusiasts and academics support and are supported by this registered charity to ensure the art is nurtured and developed throughout the UK.

Many activities of the Society are available to all, such as locating storytellers on the Society website, taking part in our annual National Storytelling Week at the start of every February, purchasing our quarterly magazine Storylines, or attending our Annual Gathering – a chance to revel in engaging performances, inspiring workshops, and the company of like-minded people.

You can also become a member of the Society to support the work we do. In return, you receive free access to Storylines, discounted tickets to the Annual Gathering and other storytelling events, the opportunity to join our mentorship scheme for new storytellers, and more. Among our great deals for members is a 30% discount off titles from The History Press.

For more information, including how to join, please visit

www.sfs.org.uk